RIPPLING **WATERS**

BJ IRONS

ISBN: 978-1-7370249-0-3

Rippling Waters is dedicated to all of my LGBTQIA+ readers.
Be bold. Be brave. Be you.

Part I

Scott

Chapter 1

"Dr. Pedrick, your husband is on line two," my technician said to me as she popped her head through the door of my office.

"Thank you, Cynthia. Tell him I'm finishing up patient charts for the day and I'll call him back in a few minutes." My focus remained on my laptop as I vigorously typed into the electronic medical record system to update the notes and diagnostics of the afternoon patients that visited today.

It was now 6:30pm. Another twelve-hour workday this week. But I knew what I was getting myself into when I went to medical school to become a cardiologist. And here I was now, Dr. Scott Pedrick, running my own practice. This was a fairly new experience for me. I had previously worked with a group of cardiologists at a medical center, but then decided to broaden my horizons and open up a new practice, where I was the sole practitioner. It took me a little over a year to have this office up and running with a full staff under me. I was finally able to see my labor come to fruition, except the hours I spent at the office were now taking its toll on my stress levels and my relationship with my husband.

However, I constantly reminded my husband, Garrett, that sacrifices needed to be made if we wanted to maintain our lavish lifestyle. We'd just bought a new home, vacationed out of the country at least twice a year, and had a great deal of expenses and debt under our belts we were catching up on. He was always frustrated when I brought this up, but I often reminded him that this was our reality.

As I finished updating my last patient's records, I checked the time on my cell phone to see how late it was. I shut down my laptop, turned off the lights in the office, set the security alarm, and made my way across the parking lot to my black Mercedes 250 CLA coupe. As I got into my car, I called Garrett.

"Hey. Sorry. I was finishing up charts. Heading home now," I informed him.

"Scott, how many times do I have to ask you to please let me know if you're staying at the office late? It's now seven and we haven't even decided on dinner yet. I've been waiting on you." I could sense the aggravation and disappointment behind his voice.

"I can't help it, Garrett. You know how busy I've been. This is nothing new. Why don't you just get food delivered from the sub-shop or something?" I asked.

"Well, I wish you would have told me that an hour ago. By the time I order it and it's delivered, it'll be eight o'clock. Christ, Scott! We need a better system here!"

I shook my head in annoyance. Does he not realize I just worked a stressful twelve-hour day? And now the minute I get off work, I'm dealing with his stress too? This was something our therapist had gone over with us God only knows how many times. Yet here I was, paying her a fortune to repeat the same lingering issues in our marriage, over and over again.

I decided to keep my cool and not add fuel to the fire. "That's fine by me, Garrett. Get me the usual. I'll be home in twenty minutes," I calmly stated.

"Whatever! Bye!" He ended the call after shouting this.

I slammed my hand hard into the steering wheel in anger. Fuck! Why does he always have to get pissed with the smallest things? He literally goes from a zero to a one-hundred in a matter of seconds.

Was all of this really worth it? The stress of work only to come home to more added stress? I continued to question all of it. My emotions were running wild and I needed to get control of myself. I took a few deep slow breaths. Inhale…exhale. I was hoping that moving into a new home, with a change of scene, would put Garrett in a better mood, and boy was I wrong. He was still being the same Garrett he had always been for the past several years.

Garrett and I have now been married for a total of five years. I'm thirty-six years old and he's thirty-two. We started dating about seven years ago, during my residency at Freemont Memorial Hospital. We actually met through an online dating app. And no, it wasn't Grindr. I have a little more couth than that.

We had our first date at an Italian restaurant. His profile picture did not do him justice. He was 5'9" and in fairly good shape. Pretty muscular. But it wasn't his body, nor his sleek and shiny brown hair, that physically attracted me to him. It was those blue-green eyes that drew me in. His eyes are beyond captivating. They look like an ocean you want to dive right into.

I'm a little taller than him at 6'0" even. Also, I'm a bit stockier and more muscular than he is too. Another distinction between us is our hair. Mine is black and starting to thin out with age, but nothing that gel and the right hairstyle can't fix. The other major difference that made us instantly compatible was the sex. He's more of a bottom and I mostly topped. So, the key fit the lock.

Maybe opposites really do attract, because he and I are polar opposites. I'm a cardiologist, while he works a typical nine to five desk job for an insurance company. And I say that not to sound pretentious or more important than him, but I say it to clarify that I am way busier than he is, where I sometimes have to go into the office for emergency patients on a weekend or have to take phone calls that interrupt our vacations and dinners out. There is not a day that goes by where Garrett doesn't remind me of this. It could even be a quick two minute phone call about a patient who is having issues and Garrett would wind up holding a two day grudge over it. *It's insane!*

I can also admit that I am more introverted than Garrett is. He is the life of the party and enjoys the attention he gets from people. He loves posting our life on Instagram, whereas I don't bother with social media, except for Facebook, where I'm only friends with my family and a few other close people. I don't have that kind of time like he does. Plus, I'm not one for needing instant gratification. I'm pretty pleased with myself, my education, job, and my status in life. I have no need to share or show it off with the rest of the world. That's just not for me. If Garrett wanted to do that, he could. And I didn't mind it at all. To each their own. It only ever becomes an issue when he asks me to take a hundred different photos of him in a single day. That's when I blow my gasket, when I feel more like his professional photographer than his actual husband. But he's learned to tame it down over the years with begging me to take his pictures. *Thank god for the invention of the selfie-stick.*

From our very first date, I could immediately recognize Garrett's playful side and fun personality. I wanted more of that positive energy in my life, so I had to see more of him. Once we had sex for the first time, which was probably the best sex of my life, our fates were sealed. Ever since, we've been inseparable, until recent years that is. I kept telling myself that every marriage has its problems, whether its gay or straight. But so far, even our therapist hasn't been able to put a dent in resolving those issues.

I pulled into the driveway of our new single, family home we purchased two months ago. It's over 4,000 square feet larger than our last home, with five bedrooms, seven and a half bathrooms, and a gym and theatre room in the basement. Garrett also demanded that our next house have an inground pool, and luckily, this one did. So, after a few negotiating bids between our realtor and the sellers, we finally settled, and we were now new homeowners.

The real reason for the move wasn't because we needed a bigger space, nor was it because we wanted more amenities. It was really to improve our relationship. Garrett and I have not been on the same page lately. Our arguments that were once non-existent, were now occurring on almost a daily basis. Not to mention our sex life went right down the drain too. When we were first married, we had sex about two to three times a week. Cut to five years later, and now it's more like once every three months or so.

We were both able to recognize our emotional and sexual distancing from each other and decided that maybe purchasing a new home would do the trick to help get us back on track. However, the results haven't changed much between us since the move, even with the added therapy. Yeah, we did have sex when we first moved in, but not as much lately.

Not to mention the stress of refurnishing, painting, and maintaining a brand, new home has also been a huge burden, mainly on Garrett. Because I'm working so much, he has more time to take care of our house. Again, this was a conversation we had before we even made the move. I told him on numerous occasions that if we did move into this home, I would have very little time to devote to work on it. However, he insisted he was fine with it and that it wouldn't be a problem. I should have known that he just said that, only being concerned with the title, status, and zip code the home brought with it, and not the actual work that was required for its upkeep.

This was another one of the recurring problems that was on the re-rinse cycle that our therapist had to listen to repetitively. Garrett was completely delusional with the entire thing. He swore that he never once claimed that he was okay with me working long hours, knowing that the burden of the house maintenance would fall mostly on his shoulders. Because of this, our therapist went into a completely different direction with how to solve this concern, when instead, the real issue was Garrett's fabrication of stories and situations that he retold her in a way that was more convenient for him.

The worst part was that she believed every word he was saying, and never saw through him.

As I entered the house, I could see Garrett with his arms crossed over his chest and a vexed expression on his face. "You forgot...didn't you?" He tried to remind me of something I had no clue about.

I raised my brow in confusion. "Forgot what?"

He let out a heavy sigh and rolled his eyes. "The medication. I'm out of Warfarin," he explained.

I placed my laptop bag on the floor and took off my shoes. "Well, why didn't you tell me earlier when we were on the phone?" I asked. "I would have run to the pharmacy to pick it up on the way home from the office."

Garrett shook his head. "Oh, I don't know, Scott. I guess I forgot. Maybe it's because I had to worry about taking a half day off from work today to get home in time for the delivery men to drop off the new basement furniture. Or maybe it's because I had to hire the landscapers, lawn mowers, and gardeners for the Spring and Summer all on my own. I mean...do I need to go on?"

Here we go again! The Garrett Pedrick tirade rears its ugly head!

I placed my hands on my hips. "Well, I don't know what you expect out of me, Garrett. I can't keep track of the amount of pills you have and when you need a refill."

"Well, you *are* the cardiologist..." He trailed off.

The irony of this. Garrett has a heart condition known as Atrial Fibrillation or AFib. His heartbeats are irregular which puts him at high risk for a stroke and heart failure. AFib onset is very rare for someone under the age of forty. So, Garrett is on blood thinners and anticoagulant medication, like Warfarin, to reduce those risks. My husband has a rare heart condition for his age, and I'm a cardiologist. It's a coincidental, yet beneficial, situation for him to have my expertise accessible to him at all times.

"Well, I can pick it up for you tomorrow, if you can hold off until then?" I suggested.

"That's fine. Thanks." He seemed less irate when he said this.

The doorbell rang to interrupt our banter. Garrett went to go answer it and grab the food, bringing it back to the kitchen island. I had to admit, I was starving, and a nice chicken Caesar salad was exactly what I was craving. Garrett on the other hand, decided on a less healthy option with his foot-long Philly cheesesteak. I sat there and silently judged him as he ate it.

He gave me an odd look, and based on that expression, I knew he could sense my disappointment with his dinner selection. Garrett rolled his eyes and could not help but smile at me. "Can you please take off the doctor hat for the rest of the night?" He requested.

I smiled back at him. "Only if you learn to act right."

Our conversation finally returned back to being light-hearted and casual. That's just the way it was with us in recent years. We could both go from yelling and bickering to a matter of laughing and being flirtatious all within minutes. Although, the scales were currently tilted more towards the argumentative side versus the fun-loving side of us.

After dinner, we decided to sit on the couch over a glass of red wine and catch up on a few television shows to unwind for the remainder of the night. Halfway through the show, I could feel Garrett's foot applying pressure to my upper leg muscle, beneath the blanket. The touches were subtle but became more noticeable when he pressed harder into it. He clearly wanted my attention, so I turned my head to face him. All I could see was a devilish grin on his face, as he raised his wine glass to his lips to take a sip of it.

I knew exactly what that look meant. Garrett was horny as hell and was ready to get fucked. As much as I wanted to have sex, I was so tired and exhausted at the moment. Not to mention I was still slightly annoyed at his irrational behavior from earlier, so that turned me off a little. I decided to give him the next best option, which was to meet him halfway.

"Honey, I'm so tired…but I wouldn't mind a blowjob," I recommended. And it was true. I could use a nice suck after the crazy day I've had at work. I really needed to release some steam.

He put his wine glass down on the coffee table and knelt down on the floor in front of me. He removed my belt, unbuttoned my pants and slowly unzipped them. I sat up on the couch slightly, to allow him to easily pull my pants down. In one fell swoop, he pulled my underwear down with them, so my slightly hardened cock was now exposed.

Garrett wrapped his hand around it and started stroking it. I closed my eyes and let out a heavy sigh of relief as I felt his skin make contact with my dick. I kept my eyes closed as he continued to motion up and down on it with his hand.

Seeing how relaxed I was, this prompted him to spit on it and place his mouth over my tip.

"Mmmm," was all that managed to escape my lips as I felt the warmth of his mouth and tongue.

His head started to bob as his slow, up and down movements, progressed into faster ones. His hand returned back to my cock along with his mouth to provide more friction and sensitivity to it. I looked down at him to see that his eyes directly locked in with mine, as Garrett was on his knees, sucking me off. I then bent my neck back so that my head was rested on the cushion of the couch, facing the ceiling, with my eyes closed.

I hated to admit this, but lately, I kept my eyes shut so I could picture a hot, younger guy servicing me. The thought of this heightened the nerve endings on my dick. I could feel the pressure starting to build up.

Garrett's dirty comments added to the pleasure. He released himself from my cock for a brief second. "Fuck yeah, Scott. Cum for me, baby!" He then returned his mouth back to its rightful place and continued blowing me more rapidly and with deep, sexy moans in between each stroke.

The combination of all these erotic gestures hitting every single one of my senses, made me ready to explode. "Fuck, Garrett. Here it comes! Argghhhh!" Just like that, I released myself hard and deep into the back of his throat. He lightly gagged, but my hands pressed the back of his head into me, so that he took all of my cum and was forced to swallow it all. As soon as I could feel he had taken every last drop, I let his head go and he sat back, taking one final gulp.

"Fuck that was good," was all I managed to say before he was leaning up to me and giving me a kiss on the lips.

I was unsure if he too needed to be satisfied in anyway or if he even wanted to be.

"Do you want me to…" I paused, assuming he knew what I was referring to.

"Nah. I'm good. But thanks for offering," he replied back to me. This led me to predict that he probably jerked off earlier today, which I was absolutely okay with. It was less extra work for me.

I pulled my pants back up and began zipping and buttoning them. It always seems awkward to start a conversation right after fucking or getting a blowjob. So, we sat silent for about a minute or so before I decided to speak. "Anything on the agenda for this weekend?" I asked.

Garrett shrugged. "Not that I'm aware of. Oh! I did plan on meeting Jess for brunch tomorrow. Shouldn't be too long though. Besides that, we have Elite Aquatics coming out to open up the pool for the summer. Speaking of which, we'll probably have to look into getting a pool guy or something in the near future."

"A pool boy?" All of my thoughts directly went to the thousands of gay pornos with hot and tan, twink pool boys I've watched over the years.

Garrett laughed at my reaction. “Yes. A pool boy! And don’t be getting any ideas!” He exclaimed.

I shook my head. “Of course not! I know how to look and not touch.”

Chapter 2

While Garrett was eating oysters and drinking bottomless Bloody Marys with his friend, Jess, for brunch, I wanted to take advantage of the quiet, alone time I had in the house. It was very rare that I had this opportunity. Usually, Garrett was always around when I was home. When he was out of the house, I was most likely working in the office.

Now that I did have this privacy and free time all to myself, I grabbed a beer out of the refrigerator and decided to turn on the fireplace in the formal living room. I plopped down in the accent chair by it and turned on my laptop, pulling up the most recent publications in the American Journal of Cardiology to skim. What can I say? Reading was very relaxing to me, and I enjoyed learning new things, especially in my field of study. I wanted to be up to date with the latest trends and research in cardiology. So, right now, I was in my own little world.

Three hours later, my concentration was disrupted as I heard the garage door open and close. It prompted me to log off my laptop and put it back in the office. By the time I made my way into the kitchen, I could see Garrett was sitting on a stool at our kitchen island, scrolling through his phone. Aware of my presence, he looked up from it at me.

"Hey," was all he said.

"Hey. How was lunch with Jess?" I asked.

He shrugged. "It was nice catching up with her. She got a new promotion. So, she's been busy with that."

"Oh! Well good for her," I enthusiastically replied.

"Yeah. What have you been up to?" He inquired.

I grabbed another beer bottle from the fridge and popped the cap while he spoke. "Nothing much. Just reading some medical journals. Boring shit."

He busted out laughing. "Yeah. Sounds pretty boring alright."

I took a sip from the bottle. "Mhmm. And while you were gone, I also booked us a reservation for dinner tonight." At the recommendation of our therapist, we should each take the time to plan out at least one romantic gesture a week. This was my contribution.

Garrett gave me a surprised look. "Oh? Where at? And what's the occasion?"

I gave a light chuckle. "No occasion. Just a normal dinner date with my husband at the Empire Garden."

He smiled at me. "Well, that sounds nice. It's been a while since we've been there."

The Empire Garden was a copacetic Chinese restaurant that served food with an Americanized twist. Garrett and I usually ordered a variety of appetizers there and devoured them, all over cocktails, whenever we went.

"Yeah. I figured we could get out for the night. Maybe hit up Ellis's Piano Bar afterwards?" I added.

He nodded. "That sounds good to me. But before that, we need to sort some maintenance issues and finances out, starting off with getting a pool boy as soon as possible, since the pool is being opened tomorrow."

I raised my brow to him. "How do you suppose we find a pool boy? Paper ads? Craigslist?"

Garrett rolled his eyes at me. "Man, you really are behind the times, Scott. You just keep out-aging yourself. Luckily, you have me here. I already took care of it."

"Took care of it? And how did you manage to do that?" I questioned him.

"Simple. I put a few posts out there on Instagram and Facebook last night, to see if anyone knew of someone wanting to be hired," he explained.

"Oh. Well, did anyone reply to them?" I asked.

"Yeah. One person did. This guy named Logan Rippling, apparently?" Garrett held out his phone to show me a picture of this Logan character.

Logan Rippling was fucking hot as shit!

He wore a skimpy, dark blue speedo, posing on a beach. He was extremely tan with a sexy six pack. His suave hair was gelled high yet looked like it was blowing in the wind at the same time. The twink looked like he was in his early to mid-twenties.

I took notice of Garrett staring at me, trying to get a sense of my reaction to the alluring pool boy he had shown me. I decided to be nonchalant about it, figuring he would get jealous if I made any compliments about him. "Is this guy even a real person?" I asked. Showing Garrett any indication of sexual desire towards this guy would turn into another side issue during our therapy sessions. I knew my husband all too well and I could see it now. He would ramble on to Dr. Williams. *Scott gives more attention to a random person on the internet, than to me!* On the inside, I was deeply irritated at the thought.

"Yes. He has plenty of photos of himself online. I thought the same thing and already investigated his profile thoroughly. I replied back to his inquiry and asked if he wanted to come over tomorrow for a quick interview and to give us an estimate for his services," Garrett added.

Well, this was moving rather fast. I still had some skepticism about this gorgeous boy and whether or not he was even a real person. But the fact that he claimed that he would be over tomorrow, would soon alleviate that worry. "Oh? And what did he say?"

"He said that's fine. He'll be over at noon tomorrow," Garrett replied.

"Cool. Sounds like a plan." I ended the conversation there and we moved on to a different subject. However, I could not get the thought of Logan out of my head. He was so fucking sexy. There was something exciting about the idea of him potentially being our pool boy for the entire summer. This led me to further thoughts about him all day.

Why was a guy that hot working as a pool boy and not as a model or fitness trainer?

Was he single or was he taken with an equally hot boyfriend?

Was he nice or was he a typical snobby twink?

I had no idea why, but I couldn't stop thinking about this boy. I had a permanent hard-on all day with thoughts of him by our pool with his wet, dripping muscles. I was a mad man, obsessed and intrigued with the idea of meeting him.

Even during dinner and at the piano bar with Garrett, I could barely give him my full and undivided attention. I tried my best to keep up with the conversations we were having and show him I was interested in everything he had to say, but my mind was completely consumed by Logan Rippling.

Once we got home, I was relieved. Garrett was completely wiped out, having fallen asleep for a short time on the car ride home. As soon as we got in the door, he made that known to me. "I'm gonna go to bed, babe. You coming up?"

I shook my head. "No. You go ahead. I'm not all that tired yet. I'll probably come up in an hour or so. Just gonna hop on the computer or watch a TV show."

He smiled at me and kissed me on the lips. "Goodnight, Scott. Tonight was…*nice*. Love you."

I kissed him back. "Yeah. It was pretty nice. And love you too."

Garrett turned back around and went upstairs. As soon as I heard the bedroom door shut, and realized he was in bed for good, I went into the office and logged onto the computer. I found myself typing *www.instagram.com* into the browser. The screen soon prompted me to type in a username and password. Luckily, I was so anal-retentive when it came to keeping track of passwords, I had a file on our computer that contained a table full of mine and Garrett's usernames and passwords for various websites and software. Even Garrett's Instagram log-in information was in this file.

I scrolled down in the document until I found what I was searching for. I switched tabs and went back to the Instagram home page and typed in GPedrick180 and the password #2Hot4U.

Really Garrett? That's your password? Really?

As soon as I was signed in, I went to the search icon and typed in Logan Rippling, and sure enough the picture of the pool boy that Garrett showed me earlier was now staring at me on my screen. I clicked on it, which took me to his profile page.

A few things stood out to me initially. The first, was his full name. Logan Ian Rippling. The second, was what his "bio section" read.

Rosé All Day! Established in 1997. Human Services Major.

Well, at least he likes rosé. So, that's not a bad thing.

I did the math in my head from 1997 until now. That meant he had to be twenty-three or twenty-four years old, which was fairly close to what I had initially guessed. Then, I thought about him being a Human Services Major. So, he wants to go into human resources or possibly the hospitality business. At least he's in college, so he can't be that dumb, right? But even if he wasn't all that bright, who would care with how gorgeous he was.

I started scrolling through his photos. A lot of them were of Logan shirtless, showing off his perfect abs, biceps, chest, and leg muscles at the beach or spread out across lounge chairs by different swimming pools. I also saw some pictures of him cooking in the kitchen, making food.

So, he cooks. Not bad, not bad.

I didn't realize the time. I had spent thirty minutes entranced with Logan's Instagram page, practically stalking the poor guy.

"Hey!" I heard a voice call.

I immediately closed out of the Instagram page in nervousness and looked up from the screen to see Garrett standing in front of me. Thank god he couldn't see the computer. He could only see the back of the monitor from where he was standing, at the entrance to the office.

"Hey. What's up?" I responded. making sure to sound as casual as possible. I tried not to look like a deer in headlights, as if I got caught doing something I wasn't supposed to.

"Nothing. Just came downstairs to grab a glass of water. Had the TV on for a bit, but I'm actually gonna go to sleep now. You coming up soon?" Garrett leaned against the frame of the white French doors to the office.

I nodded. "Yeah. Give me a second to finish up here and I'll be up."

He smirked at me. "Okay. See you soon, then." With that, he walked away and went back upstairs. As soon as he was out of sight, I let out a deep breath in relief. I then went into the browsing history of our internet and made sure to delete any trace of me being on Garrett's Instagram account and having searched Logan's profile.

This wasn't my first time at the rodeo.

But I usually never had to be secretive with my husband. The only other time I did remove any internet searches was for the porn sites I visited every now and then. I just figured it was embarrassing for me if he saw what I was searching. I was allowed to have at least that little bit of privacy, right? Even our therapist agreed that some privacy was healthy.

As soon as I could see the Instagram links were no longer there, I closed out of all the opened tabs and shut down the computer. I turned off the lights and went upstairs. Much to my surprise,

Garrett was already sound asleep. I quietly climbed into my side of the bed and got underneath the blankets, resting my head on the pillow. I stared up at the ceiling, reflecting on everything that had transpired today.

Why was I this fascinated with the pool boy? I needed to get a hold of myself. What was that quote that Garrett always used to say to me?

Oh yeah! "You need to check yourself, before you wreck yourself."

Chapter 3

I'm an early riser. On weekdays, I'm usually up between 5:00-6:00am getting ready for work and then I head into the office before everyone else arrives, reviewing my patient charts for the day. This circadian rhythm carried over into the weekends, as well. Even when I don't set my alarm for the morning, I never wake up past seven.

This Sunday morning was no different. I jogged my daily two mile run around the community. When I was finished, I lifted weights in our basement gym, before I went to take my shower, which included a nice trim and shave job. However, after I dried off and made my way into the walk-in closet, then that's when my daily routine changed.

Something wasn't quite right here. On workdays, it was easy. I usually wore a pair of dress pants, button-down shirt with a matching tie, designer shoes, etc. On normal weekends, it wasn't that difficult either. I would put on my typical leisure clothes, unless Garrett and I were expecting to go somewhere for the day. Then, I would obviously dress up for the event.

But this wasn't a normal weekend. No. Today, we were meeting and interviewing our potential sexy pool boy. I was still hesitant as to whether or not he was "catfishing" us. But remembering the multitude of pictures he had on Instagram from last night, I was more inclined to think that he would actually show up at our doorstep, at noon.

And based on this inclination, I was now worried about how I looked. Yes, I'm married and have no intention of ever cheating on my husband, but still, I wanted to make a nice first impression on

Logan. The metacognition started kicking in and I had to laugh at myself. I'm the employer and interviewer, yet I'm the one concerned with how I look and making a good impression on the guy we're interviewing? Maybe I was overthinking this whole thing. Whatever.

I decided to go with an expensive pair of designer denim jeans and black dress shoes. I then went for a black polo I absolutely loved and unbuttoned it, so it showed off my chest hair and round pecs. Not to mention the sleeves on this polo cuffed at just the right length and was tight enough to really accentuate and show off my thick arm muscles.

I gelled and brushed my hair, being fairly pleased with how I looked as I stared at myself in the bathroom mirror. With that, I returned downstairs to grab a glass of iced coffee, before I went into the office to log onto the computer to browse through news stories.

An hour later, Garrett emerged from his slumber and came into the office in his black boxer-briefs and white t-shirt. I can't discredit my husband. He does look sexy when he wakes up in the morning. His hair is messy and out of place, but it has that hot, unkempt look about it. I'll be honest, on physicality alone, I would have sex with my husband every day of the week if I could.

But when you're married, there are certain bumps in the road. Emotions and personality become part of the sex drive. And when you're not on the same page emotionally, your personalities tend to combat with each other, like mine and Garrett's were for the past few years. When this is the case, the sex starts to take a backseat in the relationship.

So, as much as I wanted to fuck the hell out of Garrett right now, with the way he looked, I couldn't bring myself to do it at this very moment.

He scratched the back of his head and yawned, while observing me. "Well, aren't you all dolled up this morning." He tilted his head to get a better view of what I was wearing.

I kept my eyes on the computer screen as I spoke to him. "I wouldn't exactly say jeans and a polo qualify as 'dolled up,' but if you're trying to say I look good, I'll accept the compliment."

I didn't have to glance up at Garrett to know that he was rolling his eyes at me. "Smart ass!" That was all he said to let me know he appreciated my quick wit and humor.

He continued on. "Well, you do have on the infamous black polo…"

Infamous black polo? Was that even a thing?

I decided to play along with him. "Infamous black polo? Do you give pet names to all of my clothes?" I asked.

He shook his head. "No. But I've only ever seen you wear that shirt when we go out to a gay club, which leads me to believe you think you look really good in it and mean to impress people. And a gay club is not on our itinerary for the day, which makes me wonder…you're trying to look good for the pool boy, aren't you?" He gave me a hardcore stare to scrutinize how I would react to his remarks.

Damn Garrett! He really did know me all too well! It was hard to get anything past him!

I busted out laughing at his question to make him think that he was being overly insecure. "Garrett…why would I feel the need to impress a pool boy?"

He shook his head. "Be real about it, Scott! You can't weasel your way out of this one. Admit it! You think he's sexy as fuck. Don't deny it. Even I can say I think he's hot."

Well, if Garrett was willing to confess that he thought Logan Rippling was hot, then there should be no need for me to hide my feelings about him too. "Fine. I'll admit, that based on the picture you showed me yesterday, yeah. He's a pretty good-looking guy."

Garrett stepped forward and stood over me, as I sat in the black leather office chair. His hovering over me, with his bulge practically in my face, did leave me feeling a bit uneasy. I felt his hand move to my shoulder, rubbing it. "A pretty good-looking guy?" He questioned. "Logan is a smoke bomb! Those abs, those muscles, that cute and innocent face of his..."

He straddled me and sat on my lap, putting his arms around my neck and intimately whispered in my ear, "Oh, come on, Scott. No need to be awkward about it. We should be secure enough to talk about this with each other. We both think the pool boy is hot as fuck. And yeah, it does turn me on a bit, but I want to take all of that sexual aggression out on you."

Well, this was a different side of Garrett I hadn't seen for quite some time. I was completely intrigued by it. This was the Garrett I fell in love with, the mischievous, frisky man who was extremely carefree about most things. Earlier, I wouldn't have even put sex as an option on the table for Garrett and me today, based on all the emotions that have been running high, but there can always be an exception to this rule, I suppose. Sometimes getting in the mood can really sneak up on you.

Now, I was really getting turned on by him, and I could feel the growth of my dick restricted to the tightness of my jeans. Garrett began unbuttoning them. But before he could get them undone, I was already grabbing him by the ass and lifting him in the air, kissing him passionately. I brushed the papers on the office desk to the side and managed to scoot the keyboard over enough to leave a clean surface, for Garrett to lay his back down on. He lifted his t-shirt over his head and threw it to the floor as I took off my polo and pulled down my pants. I lifted his legs in the air and planted a kiss on his calf muscle. He used his other leg to rub my cock with his foot.

Fucking hot as hell!

I gripped the band of his boxer-briefs, and practically ravaged them from his body, tossing them to the side. I knelt down on the ground, so my face was aligned with his ass. My tongue met his hole and he whimpered with pleasure.

His hand moved to my head, pulling and tugging on my hair as I continued to rim him. "Fuck, Scott!"

I continued to eat him out for a few minutes, before rising back up to my feet. I was ready to fuck the hell out of Garrett!

He smiled at me, knowing how sexually aroused I was. I could tell he sensed my desperation in wanting to feel the inside of that hot ass of his. "Lube's in the bottom drawer, no?" He asked.

What? How the hell did he know I kept a bottle of lube in the back of the bottom desk drawer?

Again, nothing ever gets past Garrett.

I yanked the drawer open and snatched the bottle out. I flipped the cap open and squeezed the slippery content into my hands, stroking my dick with it, before I handed the bottle off to him. He drenched his fingertips with the lube and began to finger his hole with them.

It was inevitable. My dick was ready to be plunged into that ass of his, and I wouldn't make him have to wait for it any longer. As soon as I saw him pull his fingers out from inside him, I instantly substituted my cock in their place, without warning.

Garrett let out a pleasurable yelp, at the quickness of it all. "Damn, Scott! Fuck me babe! Fuck me!" He grabbed the back of my neck and pulled me down to meet his face to kiss him. As our lips were locked, I moved my hands to grip underneath his quad muscles. As I released the kiss, I stood upright, and started plowing him. The slow movements in and out of his hole intensified and turned into faster ones. I could see his eyes were closed and his hand was on his own cock, stroking it. I moved my own hands up, grabbing his ankles, and spread his legs wide apart, continuing to fuck him.

"Yeah…that's it, babe! Right there! You ready for it!?" I asked.

"Hell yes, Scott. Give it to me! Cum in me!" He yelled.

"Fuck…here it comes! Arghhh!" I groaned heavily. My dick pulsated inside him as I jizzed deep in his hole.

His hand continued to rapidly move up and down on his own cock. "I'm gonna cum Scott! Fuck!" And just like that, he came soon after me. He shot straight up his stomach and across his chest. Damn!

Our heavy breaths slowed their pace. I pulled my cock out from him and wiped my head with my forearm. "Fuck, Garrett! That was hot!"

He let out a light chuckle. "All that talk about the pool boy really did a number on us, huh?"

I simply shrugged. "I guess it did." As I said this, I waddled my way to the laundry room to grab a towel to wipe my dick off with. I brought it back into the office to see that Garrett hadn't moved an inch, not wanting his cum to drip from his body onto our desk or carpet. I tossed the towel to him and he wiped himself down, before he rose to put his underwear and shirt back on. I proceeded to do the same with my jeans and polo shirt.

After we were both clothed, he placed his hand on my chest and kissed me once again. "Love you, babe. After that, I think I need some fresh air and probably a good iced coffee or two. Want one?" Garrett asked me.

I shook my head. "Nah. I have iced coffee here. But you can go ahead out and grab your own if you want. Thanks for asking."

"Of course," he said. He soon left the office and went back to our bedroom to get changed and then headed out the door.

This gave me time to reflect. A blowjob and sex all in one weekend? Not to mention it had only been a month or so since the last time we had sex. This time, it didn't feel like an obligation though. It felt natural. I had wanted it so bad in the moment. Maybe it was the new house that was getting our sex life back on track? Perhaps our long therapy sessions were actually working? It only took me a second to realize that this was not the case at all. It was the thought of having that pool boy around that made us horny as hell.

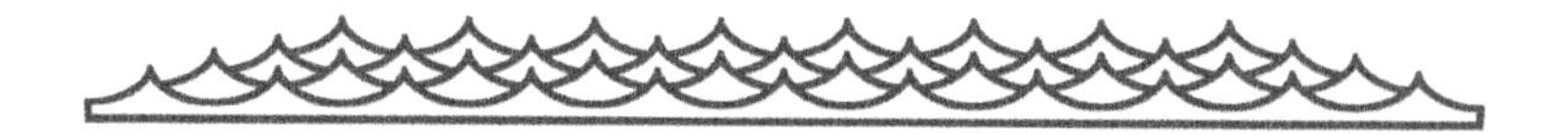

A few hours later, minutes before noon, I stood in the kitchen talking with Garrett about the plan for hiring Logan.

"So, what's a reasonable price? And we haven't even talked about how often we want him over to tend to the pool," I added.

Garrett shook his head. "Relax. I have it all taken care of. Let me do the talking and the numbers. I promise I won't put us into bankruptcy over a pool boy for Christ's sake!"

Our conversation was put to a halt at the sound of the doorbell. "That's probably him. I'll go grab it," Garrett stated, before heading to the front door to open it. I could hear them talking from the kitchen.

"Hi Logan! Nice to meet you!" Garrett greeted him with.

"Yes. A pleasure to meet you too, Garrett," I heard Logan say.

Fuck! That voice was husky and sultry! Sexy as hell! So, he is real after all!

"Welcome to our home! Why don't I take you into the kitchen? My husband, Scott, is waiting there," Garrett suggested.

"Sure! Show me the way," Logan replied.

I could hear their soft footsteps across the floor turn into louder ones, realizing they were a few feet away from entering the kitchen.

"Here he is!" Garrett introduced us the instant that Logan stepped into the kitchen. "Scott…Logan. Logan…Scott."

I blankly stared at him and offered my hand out to shake his. Luckily, he accepted it and shook it back, looking directly at me. "It's great to meet you, Scott," he stated.

"Well, it's great to meet you too, Logan," I replied back to him.

I couldn't believe it. I was in a state of awe. It was the guy I saw on Instagram, now in the living flesh. His face was carved by a Greek god. His arms were tan, and he wore a tight, baby blue t-shirt, that gave my imagination the ability to visualize that beautifully sculpted, chiseled chest and abs of his, hidden beneath it. Logan Rippling was real and there was nothing fake about him. I could not help but let my eyes wander up and down his entire body. However, I made quick work of it, hoping he wouldn't notice me checking him out.

Garrett interrupted our greeting. "So, Logan…why don't we tell you what we're looking for and you can either accept the terms or come back with a counteroffer?"

Jesus, Garrett. What was this? The television show, Shark Tank?

Logan's smile turned into a serious expression as he addressed Garrett. "Sure. That sounds good to me."

Garrett pulled out one of the stools at the island for Logan to have a seat in. Meanwhile, Garrett and I sat on the stools directly across from Logan. Garrett patted his hand on my thigh, before speaking. "Alright, then. So, we were thinking Friday afternoons, Saturday mornings, Sunday mornings, and then either Tuesday or Wednesday…whichever of those two days works best for you. Four days a week total. Shouldn't take you more than two hours a day to tend to it, right?"

Logan rubbed the bottom of his chin, deep in thought. "That sounds pretty reasonable, but do you mind if I head out back and take a look at what I'm working with, and the equipment you have?" He requested.

I decided to speak up to at least feel like I was taking part in this *interview*. "Sure. We can walk you out back. Follow us."

We all rose from our seats. Garrett and Logan followed closely behind me, heading out to the backyard. This backyard was our oasis. It had a lanai with plenty of outdoor seating and furniture. Just outside the lanai was our pool, which spanned the length of our backyard. It was fifty-two feet long with a spa and tanning ledge on one side of it. A pergola overlooked the center of the pool and emitted a waterfall, that trickled water right into it. Around the pool was a beautiful landscape of assorted stones with a diving rock. Eight lounge chairs were scattered on one side with an umbrella between each pair of chairs. Beyond the pool was nearly an acre of fenced in, luscious green grass. This backyard was a huge selling factor for us when we bought the home. It was unlike any other we came across in our real estate search.

As we stood outside, Logan made his way around the opened pool, observing it. He commented on the condition of the pool. "A little murky right now. Will definitely need to give it a shock treatment, followed by a bag or two of diatomaceous earth, depending on the size of the bag you get."

Shock treatment? Diatomaceous earth?

These were all foreign words to me. I had minimal knowledge with pool chemicals and maintenance terms. But it sounded like Logan at least knew what he was doing and talking about. He moved to the side of the yard to get a good look at the pool pump, electrical panels, and pipes. He bent down to turn some of the valves on and off, to see the waterfall mechanisms we had that flowed into the pool. "Looks pretty good here," he stated.

Hell yeah, it looks pretty good here!

Garrett and I had the perfect view of that sexy, round, bubble butt of his as he stood in front of us, bent over, testing the equipment. Garrett abruptly elbowed me in the side, bringing me back to reality. "Alright. Obviously, we will need to purchase the shock treatment and diatomaceous earth, among other chemicals. Scott and I will run out to the store today to pick all of that up. Leave us a list of anything else you think we will need, and we will go ahead and grab it."

Logan stood back up and turned to face us. "Awesome. Yeah. Would it be easier for me to text it all to you?"

A text? We were getting his phone number already?

Well, of course we would be exchanging phone numbers. Duh! What the fuck else did I expect? If he would be working for us, then yeah, we would definitely be needing that. I simply didn't bother to consider it until now.

Garrett pulled out his cell phone from his pocket. Once he unlocked it, he handed it off to Logan. "Here. Add yourself to my contacts and then I'll shoot you a text, so you have my number," he explained.

Well that wasn't right. Garrett would have Logan's number and vice versa, but what about me? I decided to interject, handing him my phone too. "In case of an emergency, and Garrett's unavailable, just give me your number as well." As I said this, I hoped that it didn't come off as too abrasive to either one of them.

But seeing Logan smile at me, instantly made me melt on the inside. Based on this reaction of his, I presumed he didn't think I was being weird or anything. "Sure. No problem, Scott." He typed his number into my phone as well. I then shot him a text.

Scott Pedrick. This is my number.

Garrett chimed in. "Well, I guess now would be a good time to discuss how much we can pay you. Zero dollars and zero cents an hour." My husband laughed at his own joke. "No. I'm teasing. Well, let's average it to a generous two and a half hours for four days a week. So, roughly ten hours, weekly. Does two hundred dollars a week sound reasonable, starting this week?"

What? Two hundred dollars for four days a week? There is no way that…

Logan replied right away. "Yeah. That sounds good to me."

Woah! I was surprised that he accepted that offer. I was thinking we would be having to pay him at least five-hundred dollars a week, at minimum. This was a complete steal! This hot pool boy came rather cheap.

Garrett and Logan shook hands to solidify the deal, before Garrett spoke up. "Great. I'll have a formal contract typed up and signed by all three of us. And how do you prefer we pay you? By check, PayPal, Venmo…?"

Logan nodded. "I'm good with Venmo."

It was all settled. We had officially hired a suave, steamy pool boy for the summer. I don't know what was steamier: the pool boy, or the thoughts in my head about him.

Chapter 4

It had been two weeks since we hired Logan Rippling as our pool boy. Garrett and I were not upset with this *investment.* Logan was a hot distraction for me as I worked in my office during the weekends. I would catch myself checking him out through the office window that faced the backyard, while he skimmed and tended to the pool. This was the best location for me to watch him, without Garrett catching me.

Much to my disappointment, Logan had not once taken off his shirt since he started working for us. He usually wore a thin t-shirt or tank top and low-cut swim trunks. At least I was able to see his sexy, tan legs and feet. I especially took notice whenever he bent over to clean out the filters.

His ass was out of this world. My fucking god!

The following Saturday, Garrett and I had planned our housewarming party with our closest gay friends. We limited it to ten people, besides us. We weren't too crazy of partiers, but we wanted to make sure we still had a good time and kept the drinks flowing. So, we had three coolers outside, full of canned spiked seltzers, soft drinks, and beers. We kept the wines and liquor bottles in the lanai, with tons of food, appetizers, and snacks across the outdoor table.

Everyone began to arrive. Our good friend, Pete, and his partner, Lyle, came first. Pete has been my good friend for years. We go way back to medical school. He is now an ophthalmologist, while his fiancée, Lyle, works for him as a front office manager for their practice. This was something I had tried to convince Garrett to do for the past year and a half. I wanted him to work in my office with me. I figured it would be something that would bring us closer together. Because success of the practice dictated our primary income, I thought Garrett would want his hands in it, as well.

However, Garrett was having none of it. He claimed that it would make me his boss and that it would wind up ruining our marriage. He also explained that he wanted to continue working at the insurance company, because that was something that was solely his, that he did for himself, and that I had no control over.

Over the past several years, I could see a change in my husband. He developed an *inferiority complex*, comparing my job to his. He couldn't stand that I was the breadwinner in the relationship, and he even went so far as to assume that everyone overlooked what he brought to our relationship. He cared too much about what other people thought. And he thought they viewed him as being *unworthy* of me. It was always a constant battle he brought up in our heated arguments.

His temper became short-fused over the years. Every time we ever had a slight disagreement, he would turn it into a full-fledged argument and say how he feels inadequate and how I'm the success of the relationship as the cardiologist. He would further explain that I make him feel *less* than me, when in reality, it was his insecurities leading him to these irrational thoughts.

This was never the case at all. In fact, I constantly walked on egg-shells around Garrett. I made sure that I never went out of my way to talk about my job, salary, or finances with him. I knew that would upset him and make him feel even more insecure. However, he always found a way to bring those feelings to light during our arguments.

It was now getting to the point where I started to no longer care about how he felt about this. I was constantly being positive with him, by trying to build him up. Yet he always found a way to tear himself down and to victimize himself, making it seem like I was purposefully causing him to have these feelings. Clearly, this was a him issue and it was out of my hands. It would be something he would need to deal with on his own, and right now, he was not dealing with it in the right manner. It was all taking a heavy toll on our relationship, as a result.

My thoughts on this were interrupted as Pete patted me on the back. "How you doing, Scotty? How's the practice going?"

I swallowed my Corona Light before speaking to him. "It's been going well. We are finally fully-staffed, and things seem stable now. I'm hoping my extended hours dwindle down soon."

"Well, good luck with that. I don't think I've ever worked under ten hours a day for the past two years," Pete informed me.

I shrugged and decided to change the subject, realizing that Lyle and Garrett were approaching us. I knew the last thing Garrett wanted to hear or talk about at our house-warming pool party was my work.

"So, Pete. Can I get you a drink?" I asked.

He nodded. "Sure. Can I get a scotch on the rocks?"

I laughed. "Woah! It's only noon. Starting out kind of heavy this early?"

Pete chuckled at my judgment. "With the week I had...yeah, I'll take it."

I made my way into the house to grab him a plastic tumbler and filled it with ice, before pouring the scotch into it. Garrett and I made clear rules that no one was to have any glass outside, during the party. We know how the gays get at parties and we were ninety-nine percent sure there would be some sort of drink spill by the end of the night. So, it was better to be safe, than sorry.

Our other guests arrived soon after and now the party really had begun. Everyone had their shirts off and were in low-cut bathing suits and speedos. Shots were passed around and Garrett did a toast to brag about our new house and how lucky we were to have found it, before the shots went down.

As soon as we finished the shots, I looked over to the opposite end of the yard. A young guy with navy shades came in, through the back gate. He had on a pair of dark-blue speedos. As he approached us, I could make out the curves of his body and how muscular and toned he was. Did Garrett hire an Andrew Christian model for the party that I didn't know about? This guy was fucking phenomenal!

Everyone also turned around, noticing the walking piece of sex cross the yard, towards us. Now if only we had our sprinkler system on and "Moving in Stereo" by the Cars playing, with this sexy man in slow-motion. It would have been a gay reenactment from the pool scene of Fast Times at Ridgemont High. Those thoughts dissipated as the hot guy got closer to us. I realized, it was Logan, our pool boy. Garrett walked over to him and put his arm around his shoulder, escorting him over to our group.

"Hey, everyone! This is our new pool boy, Logan!" Garrett exclaimed. He went around and introduced Logan to all our friends, before bringing him over to me.

What was he even doing here?

I sure as hell didn't invite Logan over. Actually, in last speaking with Garrett, he told me he let Logan know we were having our pool party and that he could have the day off. So, I was completely shocked that he was here right now. But I was more surprised... well, *pleasantly* surprised, to see him in a pair of speedos. Every one of our friends was eye-fucking the shit out of him, including me.

Logan took his sunglasses off to greet me. He leaned in for a hug. This caught me completely off-guard, but I accepted it, and hugged him back. A chill creeped up my spine, as I felt his body pressed against mine. I could feel the softness and silkiness of his skin with my hand that was wrapped around his back for the hug.

As we separated, he smiled at me. "Hey, Scott. Thanks for having me over."

I played along with it. "Oh. Of course. Glad you could make it."

I didn't want to seem rude and ask how he was invited. I could easily put two and two together, figuring that it was Garrett who wound up inviting him over. I just wished Garrett had mentioned this to me, so I could have been better prepared. I darted my gaze to my husband, who had an impish grin on his face. That said it all.

Garrett walked over to the two of us. "Here! Have a shot, Logan!" He gave the small Dixie cup to Logan, who drank it.

Logan gave a sour look afterwards, seeming like he wasn't expecting something that strong. I chuckled at how cute his reaction was.

"What was in that!?" He asked.

Garrett cracked up at him. "It's a secret. But yeah. Feel free to help yourself to whatever. We have coolers full of drinks out here, but the wine and hard liquor are in the screened in porch."

Logan nodded. "Great! I think I'll start off with a beer. Don't want to get too crazy, since I have to drive home later."

This response from Logan actually impressed me. Most gay guys his age wouldn't even care about their alcohol intake at a party. They assumed they would crash and spend the night at the party house, have one of their friends drive them home, or simply call and have an Uber come to pick them up, willing to come back and grab their car the following day. It was refreshing to see that Logan was not like that. He seemed responsible, with a good head on his shoulders.

Garrett patted Logan on the back again. "Ahhh! Don't worry about that! We have four guest bedrooms you can pick from, if you need to stay the night. Don't hold back!" Garrett stated, peer-pressuring Logan.

Like I mentioned earlier, Garrett was definitely the life of every party, and wanted to make sure everyone was having a great time, along with him.

Logan scratched the back of his head, seeming a little unsure of himself. "Ummm? I'll consider it. But thank you for the offer."

Then, before you knew it, that was the end of my chat with Logan. Other guys at the party were pulling him in their direction, on the lounge chairs, in the pool, etc., wanting to get the scoop on who the new twink was. It would be some time before I had my own chance to talk with Logan, one on one, and really get to know him on a more personal level.

No matter what conversation I was in with someone, I felt my attention always drifting off to see where Logan was and what he was up to. He was by far the hottest guy here at the party, and evidently, everyone else was aware of that too with how flirty they were being with him. However, I could sense an innocence within Logan. He politely laughed at people's jokes even when they weren't exactly funny, and his face turned beet red whenever anyone made a sexual innuendo at him or rubbed his chest and abs. I found myself getting a bit annoyed whenever one of my friends did rub him or touch him inappropriately, whether it was meant to be in jest or not.

Finally, seeing that Logan was soaking in the sun in one of our lounge chairs by the pool, with no one around, I decided to make my way over to him, and plopped myself down in the chair that was beside him. "So, hopefully our friends aren't causing any trouble for you?" I asked him.

He turned his head to face me, although I couldn't tell if he was directly looking at me, since he had his navy shades on. "Oh no! Not at all! Everyone's been nothing but nice to me. You have a great group of friends."

"Well, that's good. Let me know if anyone does give you any sort of issue. I'll be sure to let them have it!" I stated.

He laughed at what may have seemed like me being a little over-protective of him. "Roger that! I'll be sure to let you know." He took a sip from his red-solo cup which had some pink liquid in it. I assumed it must have been a mixed drink.

But my gaze focused on his lips that were sipping on it. I was close enough to finally be able to take notice and appreciate those lips of his. They were so luscious and smooth. Logan definitely had some sexy DSLs. I'm sure anyone who experienced those lips of his on their dick must have felt like they were in heaven.

I decided to ask him more questions about his personal life to get to know him more. "So how long have you been a pool boy for?"

"Well pool 'boy' is a bit of a stretch. I'm twenty-three, so I'm not exactly a *boy*." He added.

Oh damn! Did I insult him?

I was immediately apologetic. "My bad. Pool *guy*, then? Does that work?"

He snickered. "Haha. That works. No big deal. But yeah. I've only worked on pools for about over a year now. It's just something part-time, while I'm in college."

Well, of course. I already knew this. From the information I gathered from his Instagram account, I knew he was a Human Services Major, but I decided to ask him about it, to make it seem like I was completely oblivious. "Nice. What college do you go to? What are you studying there?" I asked.

"I'm at the local community college. This is my second year there as a Human Services Major. I'll probably transfer to a University for my last two years to obtain my bachelor's degree," he replied.

"Well, that's very smart of you. You save a ton of money by going to community college for your first two years, before transferring out," I complimented him.

He nodded. "Yeah. That was the intent. I'd rather not end up in complete financial debt by the time I graduate. Don't want to be paying back student loans while I'm in my thirties."

I had to give Logan Rippling a lot of credit. The more I heard him speak, the more mature I realized he was, for his age. He had smarts and looks. What a lethal combination.

"So, tell me about yourself," Logan inquired. "I think I heard Garrett mention that you're a doctor? What area of medicine?"

"Cardiology. I run my own practice as a cardiologist. We opened it up a year ago. It's been stressful getting it up and running, but I think we've passed that curve, and everything should be smooth sailing from here on out," I explained.

"Oh, cool! Well, if you're ever looking for a human resources manager, let me know. I will definitely be looking for a job after graduation," he stated.

"I will be sure to keep that in mind," I said.

I'm not so sure how much of a good idea that would be. I don't think I could picture Logan Rippling being my front office manager. I would be so distracted from my patients, by staring at him in his cute scrubs all day. I would wind up making some sort of mistake in the office with him being a constant distraction to me. Malpractice and negligence would be inevitable!

Garrett walked over to us and sat on the edge of the lounge chair I was in, interrupting our discussion. He held two shots out to me and Logan. "Here! You both have been slacking on me!" He exclaimed.

Logan laughed at Garrett. "I'm not sure if that's a good idea. I don't think I'd be able to drive home if I took one more."

Garrett slapped him on the leg. "Of course, you can have another shot! Our offer still stands. You can stay the night if you can't drive home. Right, Scott?"

I had to think about this for a second. Garrett was clearly drunk, and I could already feel a buzz coming on, from my end. Garrett was being a little aggressive with wanting Logan to spend the night. But I decided to not think much of it, and just went along with the plan. "Yeah. Feel free to stay over if you need to, Logan."

Logan smiled at both of us and removed his sunglasses, placing them on the top of his head. They revealed his beautiful blue-green eyes. They looked nearly identical to Garrett's, which were beyond captivating. Logan grabbed one of the shots out of Garrett's hand. "Well, if you insist. Bottoms up!" He took the shot whole. I grabbed the other drink from Garrett and did the same.

Yeah. Bottoms up!

So, Logan would be spending the night at our house. I could not help but continue to stare up and down at his exposed body for the rest of the day. I would be thinking about his hot ass, *bottom up,* for the remainder of the night.

Chapter 5

The party continued for the rest of the day. Around 8:00pm, some of the guys left, while others were starting to congregate inside the house. We had a huge bar in the basement with a karaoke mic stand. Give the gays a microphone and a bar and you have yourself an entertaining night in the making.

Eventually everyone else dried off, changed clothes and made their way downstairs. Lyle immediately turned on the television monitor and synced the karaoke system to it, ready to sing. I needed a few more drinks in me before I would consider getting up on that stage. It wasn't going to happen while I was sober. That was for sure.

Pete and I sat next to one another on the leather sofa, waiting for Lyle to queue himself up and start the performance. Garrett then came over to Pete and me, giving me a mixed drink. As he sat down beside me, he gave me a peck on the cheek. "Here, babe," he offered, handing me the glass of bourbon with ice.

"Thanks, Gare." I squeezed his upper leg a few times to show him my thanks.

I saw Lyle waving his hand in the air, as if beckoning someone to come to him. I turned my head around to see who exactly he was waving to. It was then that I saw Logan walking over to him. Logan had on a pair of gray shorts and a tight black t-shirt. His hair still looked damp from recently getting out of the pool.

I studied him for a moment, while he stood on the stage with Lyle. I was hoping he would still be in a speedo so I could continue to get a glimpse of his perfect body, but I would have to settle with this for now. At least I was still able to admire his legs and feet.

Now, I'm not the type of guy that typically has a foot fetish, but Logan did have really sexy feet. That was just a fact that no one could argue against. Seemed to be about a size nine, very tan, and looked well maintained. Who the fuck was I kidding? Logan had a perfect *everything*. There was no denying it.

Lyle wrapped his arm around Logan as the song started playing on the screen with the lyrics popping up. *Separate Ways* by Journey? Well, this was an interesting choice. Lyle must have really been drunk to start off with this one. I began laughing at how dramatic Lyle and Logan were being on stage, as they belted out a few of the notes to the song. Both were completely off key. So, maybe Logan wasn't exactly perfect at *everything*, after all.

Logan was shifting his gaze around the room, looking from the television screen to Lyle, and then back to us spectators on the couch, as he sang: "*If he ever hurts you, true love won't desert you. You know I still love you. Though we touched and went our separate ways.*"

Did Logan wink in my direction while he sang this? I could have sworn he did, but maybe it was my imagination. Or if he did, he was most likely being playful. Either way, it was cute.

Pete whispered to me. "I'm going to go grab a drink at the bar. Care to join me?"

"Sure," I replied. He and I then got up from our seats and headed over to the bar, across the room. Pete went behind the bar to grab a glass tumbler and some ice, using the bottle of scotch to pour himself a drink. I sat on one of the bar stools across the counter from him. I placed my glass of bourbon on one of the nearby coasters on our beige, granite countertop.

I spun around on the stool to still be able to watch Lyle and Logan continue singing the remainder of the song. Pete held his drink in the air, wanting me to clink my glass with his, which we did. "Here's to dealing with patients during the day and having the *patience* to listen to this caterwauling all night," he wittily said.

I chuckled at his comment. "I couldn't agree with you more on that one!" We took a swig of our drinks.

Pete leaned over the counter to bring himself closer to my ears, making sure no one else was able to eavesdrop in on our conversation. "So, I see everyone here seems to be getting along with your pool boy."

I acknowledged him. "Yeah. He's a nice and friendly guy."

Pete and I glanced over at Logan, who now went to sit on the couch once he was finished his performance with Lyle. "Not to mention, he's sexy as hell," Pete added.

I was surprised at how outright he was. I knew Lyle would have a cow if he heard Pete saying this, which made sense as to why Pete pulled me to the bar to have this discussion, away from everyone else.

"Yeah. I mean…hell, he could be a model, if he wanted to," I said.

Pete agreed with me. "Totally. So, have you and Garrett taken advantage of the opportunity, with him being your pool boy and all?"

I was not used to this side of Pete. He usually presented himself as the prim and proper doctor, which carried over into his social life, as well. He was prudish as hell, so hearing him now refer to sex, was a complete surprise.

"What? No way. Garrett and I wouldn't do that…" I trailed off.

I wanted to explain to Pete that this would be wrong on so many levels for us, but I felt awkward about divulging my marital problems with my friends. I knew there was no way Garrett would wind up going along with this. And if he did, I somehow knew it would turn into some form of disaster that would be a new hot topic at our therapy sessions.

Pete smiled in Logan's direction when he spoke. "I mean, you can't knock it, until you try it, Scott. All I'm saying is if Lyle and I had him as our pool boy, we would have definitely had a conversation by now about bringing him into our bedroom."

Woah! Now Pete was really crossing the line here. But I had to admit, Logan brought those thoughts of carnal pleasure out in everyone. Garrett and I experienced that firsthand, with the hot sex we had in the office recently, thinking about Logan.

I had to think about what Pete had suggested. Garrett and I had chats in the past about the idea of opening up our relationship to invite a third person into our sex life, for fun of course. But other than that, we were remaining monogamous. However, the opportunity of getting a third person in our bedroom that we both were sexually attracted to never presented itself since.

I remembered Garrett admitting that he thought Logan was also sexy as fuck. I wondered what he would say if I suggested that we have a three-way with him. Then, there was the flipside to that, that I didn't really consider either. What if Logan wasn't interested in having sex with the two of us? I mean, look at him. He could practically have sex with any guy he wanted, so why would he want to waste his time with us?

As I thought this, I still pictured having Logan naked in my bed. What I would do to be able to have my cock buried inside him. To be able to see that innocent, twinkish face of his moaning, enjoying every inch of my dick, was enough to give me a hard-on, right now.

I returned my attention back to Pete, but played it cool with my feelings about Logan. "Well, I guess Garrett and I could always talk about it, but I doubt anything will come of it. Besides, he's our pool boy. There's a certain respect and professionalism we should have with him, right?" I checked with Pete, wanting his verification.

Pete shrugged. "I don't think so. If anything did go south after you messed with him, well…there are plenty of other pool boys out there. Logan isn't the first, and certainly wouldn't be the last," he added.

I guess what Pete was saying made sense to me. But there was one thing he was absolutely wrong about. Yes, Logan probably wasn't the only guy looking for a job as a pool boy, but he sure as hell was the hottest one I've seen in my entire life. Better than the fake pool boys I've seen in pornos.

I swiveled back around in my stool to face Pete once again. "Well..."

My reply to him was interrupted as Lyle came over to us. "Alright, you two. Enough with the hiding. You're not getting away without having to sing tonight. Come on, Pete. Let's do our favorite."

Pete and I were forced to end our private talk, and so, we returned to the main group. The night continued with more karaoke singing, drinking, and Garrett being generous with the rounds of shots. I was pretty drunk by the time midnight rolled around. Everyone was beginning to head home, with Pete and Lyle being the last ones to leave. That left Garrett, Logan, and me upstairs, standing around the kitchen island.

Logan started yawning. "I think I'm gonna call it a night. I went ahead and put my bag and clothes upstairs in the green guest bedroom, if that's cool with you guys?"

Garrett chimed in before I could respond. "Yeah. That's fine. Have a good night, Logan. Let us know if you need anything."

"Will do. Night, Garrett. Night, Scott. Again, thanks for inviting me over today and letting me stay the night. I had a blast." Logan stood up and proceeded to head upstairs, slightly stumbling. Clearly, he was a little more drunk than I had imagined.

"Yeah. Of course. We all had a fun time. Good night," was all I said to him. He turned around to head upstairs. Garrett and I waited to hear his bedroom door shut before we decided to talk with each other.

"So, what did you think?" Garrett asked me.

"Think of what? The party?" I wasn't sure exactly what he was referring to.

"No. The party was fine. Duh. I'm talking about Logan. What did you think of him?" Garrett said, in a slightly vexed tone.

I shrugged. "He was nice and got along with everyone in our group," was all I said.

Garrett rolled his eyes at me. Clearly, he wanted me to elaborate a little more. "Well, I caught you staring at him quite a number of times, outside by the pool earlier, when he was in his sexy little speedo," he accused.

Maybe it was the alcohol that was now taking control, but I decided to be a little more open with Garrett on the subject. "Yeah. I think it's safe to say that everyone was drooling over him tonight. He's the shiny new toy that no one can have," I explained.

Garrett had a puzzled look on his face, but then it turned into a devious grin. "Well, who says no one can have him?" He questioned me.

I knew where Garrett was going with this and I was reminded of the conversation Pete and I had by the bar earlier when we talked about the possibility of Garrett and me exploring the option to have sex with Logan. It was something I was considering more and more as the night progressed and as my alcohol intake also increased. "Are you saying, you think we should…with Logan?" I asked.

Garrett smiled and moved closer to me, putting his arm around my waist. "I mean, I'm not opposed to that idea. I think it would be pretty fucking hot. Don't you?"

I nodded. "Yeah. That would be hot, but who says he's into us like that?" I questioned.

Garrett gave me a wink. "Well, I have a hunch he actually is into us. I caught wind of him staring at us shirtless, on several occasions today."

"Really? I didn't notice that. But how would we approach him about it, without being awkward?" I asked Garrett.

He thought about this for a brief moment, before answering me. "Let's give him subtle hints here and there, and we'll see what happens."

"Well, how do we do that?"

"Leave that part to me. Come on. Follow me." Garrett grabbed my hand and was soon dragging me up the stairs. He knocked on the guest bedroom door that Logan was staying in.

Shit! Was Garrett really going to outright ask Logan if he wanted to have sex with us!?

I silently stood behind Garrett and observed him. Logan opened the door simply wearing a pair of silky, tight black underwear. I could see his entire bulge right through them. It didn't leave much to the imagination. "Hey guys, is everything okay?" He asked.

Garrett leaned against the door frame. "Yeah. We're fine. We wanted to let you know we were heading to bed now too. Let us know if you *need anything*. Help yourself to going downstairs if you need to get something to eat or drink. Our kitchen and pantry are all yours for the taking."

Logan rubbed his hand through his hair, swaying it back. "Thanks. I appreciate it. Yeah. Can't think of anything off the top of my head I may need, but if I do, I know where to find you."

"No problem. Good night now." Garrett turned away to head across the hall to our bedroom and I followed as Logan shut his door behind him.

Garrett and I brushed our teeth, stripped down, and hopped in bed, turning on the lamps that were on the nightstands beside us. "So? That was your 'subtle hint?'"

He nodded. "Yup. That's the best I could do for now." Garrett rolled on top of me, pressing his chest into mine, passionately kissing me. "Goodnight babe," he stated, releasing his lips from mine.

"Goodni…" was all I was able to get out before I heard a knock at our bedroom door.

Garrett sat up, still on top of me, and yelled, "Doors unlocked. Come on in."

Our master bedroom door opened, and there stood Logan Rippling, sexy as hell in his black Calvin Kleins. "Hey, I was gonna ask if I could… Oh!" His eyes widened, realizing that Garrett was sitting on top of me in what seemed like a compromising position. He continued to speak. "My bad. I didn't realize you two were…"

Garrett interjected. "Were what? Fucking?"

Logan's voice dropped. He looked a little embarrassed. "Yeah. Fucking..."

Garrett then clarified. "No. We weren't. But…we were about to."

Logan stood still, staring at us dumbfounded, not moving an inch. "Oh, okay…"

Garrett looked down to smile at me before glancing back over his shoulder at Logan, who was still standing in the doorway. "You know you're more than welcome to watch if you want."

What!? What was Garrett saying!? Was this really happening?

Logan looked behind him for some odd reason, as if he thought someone was spying on him. He soon took a few steps forward into our bedroom, "I mean…if you both are okay with it. Yeah. I'll watch for a bit."

He shut the door behind him and moved to sit on the white accent chair in the corner of our bedroom. Logan leaned back in the chair and stretched his legs out, while spreading them. I could see him start to rub his cock through his underwear.

Meanwhile, Garrett pulled the blankets from us, exposing our nude bodies to Logan. Garrett leaned back down to kiss me on the lips. He slowly rocked his hips against me, pressing his hands into my chest.

Even while Garrett continued to kiss me, we both kept looking over to see Logan's reaction. Logan was now pulling down his underwear and flicked them off with his feet. His dick was hard as a rock, and he began to stroke it. It was thick and had a decent length to it. Roughly eight inches, I estimated.

Logan then started to groan as he pumped himself. His eyes were locked with mine. As soon as they were, he gave me a wink and had a wily smirk across his face. I was desperate in this very moment. I needed to touch him. I needed to feel his cock, his ass, his entire body on me. Garrett saved my desperation, by waving for Logan to come over to us.

Logan did as he was instructed and made his way over to our bed. He got on his knees while at my side and began kissing Garrett on the lips. I placed my hand on Logan's back and rubbed it up and down. As I did this, Logan took his own hand and placed it on top of mine. He moved it down, forcing my hand to grab and hold one of his bubbly ass cheeks.

Fuck! His ass was so soft and at the same time, muscular as hell!

I kept squeezing it and then traced my hand around to the other cheek to give it some attention as well. Garrett and Logan soon stopped kissing, and then, Logan leaned over to place his lips on mine. I was finally getting the chance to experience those luscious, rosy lips of his. His tongue started wrestling mine as we made out. Garrett moved in so that all three of us were kissing. Our tongues wrapped around one another as we continued.

I closed my eyes, allowing myself to get completely lost in this erotic fantasy that was now a reality. Once we pulled away, Garrett rolled over to lay down next to me on the bed. Logan scooted over so that he was now kneeling in between Garrett and me, hovering over the two of us. With both of his hands, he reached down to grab our cocks, stroking them.

"Oh, Fuck!" I heard Garrett whimper. A smile creeped across Logan's face when he said this. I took this opportunity to feel every square inch of Logan's chest and stomach as he faced us. Garrett's hands also navigated as much of Logan's body that was within his reach.

Logan leaned down towards me, continuing to jerk the both of us off. He kissed me once again, but this time, he bit my lower lip and moved his head towards my neck, licking and kissing it sensually. His tongue traced down the center of my chest and torso until it was merely centimeters away from my dick. I'd waited for this moment and I couldn't believe it was actually happening.

Logan was going to suck me off.

He didn't make me wait long. I felt his mouth and tongue tease the tip at first, before he dove right down on the entire length of it. "Mmmm. My god," I uttered. Logan was sensational. He moaned heavily, while blowing me. Garrett turned his head to make out with me as Logan continued sucking me off. However, as Garrett did kiss me, I couldn't help but find myself keeping my eyes open and focused on Logan. Every time Logan opened his eyes to glance up at me as his mouth moved up and down on my dick, it was enough to almost make me nut, with that beautiful, god-like face of his staring deep into my soul as he serviced me.

I tugged on his hair and pulled him up for a moment. "Shit...I don't want to cum just yet. But keep doing that, and you'll get me there," I announced.

Garrett and Logan both snickered at my reaction. So, Logan moved to the side to now give Garrett's cock some attention with his mouth.

Now that we were all here together in this very moment, I knew there would be no going back, so I let my sexual urges take over and did whatever I pleased. I leaned over to the side of the bed and stretched my arm, to open the bottom nightstand drawer, pulling out the bottle of lube. I moved to the foot of the bed and knelt behind Logan, while he continued to slurp on Garrett's dick. I now had his hot ass, bent over, in front of me, and it was mine.

All fucking mine!

I forced his legs to spread more apart with my hands, aggressively, and pushed him forward so that his back arched and his ass was high in the air, facing me. I went to town on it, like a wild maniac. My tongue and lips traced over his hole and dug in and out of it. His hole was so fucking smooth and tasted amazing. I could see that Logan had now paused from blowing Garrett. His head was twisted to get a glance of me, over his shoulder, eating him out. I could feel his hand press on the back of my head, wanting me to get deeper into his asshole.

"Fuck Scott! Don't fucking stop! I could let you do this to me all night!" Logan exclaimed. Garrett chuckled at Logan's remark and sat up to kiss him on the lips, while he was getting rimmed.

Now that I had relaxed Logan's ass up a bit, I pulled my head away and knelt up. I opened the bottle of lube and poured the liquid content onto my dick. I began stroking it to lather it up. I poured a second round of lube on the tips of my fingers and began to massage the crack of Logan's ass up and down, before my fingers circled his hole.

Logan whimpered, knowing what was about to come. Then, he let out a yelp once my index finger was inside him. At first, I wasn't sure if he was in pain or if he was enjoying it, so I started off slowly, moving my finger in and out. "How does that feel?" I asked, checking in with him.

"Phenomenal! That feels fucking amazing! I want your dick inside me! Please! Give it to me, Scott. Fuck!" Logan begged.

As he pleaded, I added a second finger in his hole to loosen it up as much as possible. I was ready to give it to him, and clearly, he was ready for it too. I knelt up and smacked my dick against his ass cheeks before pressing the tip of my cock against his hole. I rubbed it up and down his crease to tease him a bit. Soon enough, I positioned it straight on and slowly plunged myself into him. At first, it was so tight and took a bit of pressure to get the tip in. Soon, my shaft slipped in and fully immersed itself inside of him.

"Damn boy! You're tight as hell. Holy shit!" I cried out.

Logan wiggled his hips slightly, to make sure my dick was fully inside of him. I started to fuck him at a moderate pace. The feeling of being inside him was out of this world. It was pure and utter ecstasy. I wanted to be inside him forever. I never wanted to escape from it.

I wrapped my hands around Logan's hips and continued thrusting myself into him. Garrett sat up and knelt, so that Logan's mouth was aligned with his cock. He grabbed Logan by the head and pressed his face into him, with Logan now sucking Garrett off, once again, while I continued to fuck him, doggy-style. Logan was being spit-roasted by us and loving every second of it. He became more verbal, and dirtier, expressing how turned on he was. Garrett leaned forward to passionately kiss me as Logan was bent over between us, getting his brains fucked out.

It was all happening so fast. I couldn't control it any longer. "Fuck… I'm gonna cum any second. Where do you want me to cum?" I asked.

Logan pulled his mouth away from Garrett's cock to speak. "Fuck yeah, baby! Cum in me! I want every drop of your cum inside me! Breed me, daddy!" He begged.

Fuck! I loved being called Daddy! That sexy voice from this gorgeous, fit boy did it for me!

"Arghhhhhh!!! Fuckkkkk!!!" I yelled. His tight ass muscles drained every bit of my cock. I shot so deep inside of him. Then, I could hear Garrett howl. It must have been enough for him too, because he was now cumming inside Logan's mouth, as Logan gagged on his dick.

"Fuck! I'm gonna cum! I'm gonna cum! Shit! Mmmmm!" Logan screamed, releasing himself all over our bedsheets.

My thrusts inside Logan tapered off. Garrett soon pulled himself out of Logan's mouth. As I removed myself from being inside him, we all flopped down on the bed, laying down with our heads against the pillow, panting heavily.

Logan laid right in the middle, between Garrett and me. After a minute or so of us catching our breaths, it was Logan who sat up in the bed. "So…should I go back to my bedroom now?" He asked us.

I wrapped my arms right around him and pulled him back down into the pillow. "And miss out on a post-sex cuddle? I don't think so." I replied, jokingly.

Garrett rubbed his hand up and down Logan's body in a soothing manner. "Yeah. You can sleep here with us if you want. No big deal," he reassured him.

Logan let out a heavy sigh of relief. "Good. Because I'm all about the cuddling afterwards too."

We were all on the same page with this. Garrett and I reached over to the lamps by our nightstands and turned them off. It was lights out. I wrapped my arms around Logan to hold him for the night. He was my little spoon, and I loved every second of feeling his warm body against mine. Garrett also held Logan, while facing him.

I closed my eyes and tried to fall asleep. I couldn't believe that Garrett and I had our first threesome. In the seven years we have been together, this was the first. More so, I couldn't believe I just fucked the hell out of our pool boy, Logan. The incredible, Logan Rippling! I still thought I was in some sort of fantasy and that I was dreaming. I didn't want to wake up from it.

But really, I didn't want this moment to ever end. I could fuck and cuddle Logan every night if I had the chance to. And who knows, maybe this wouldn't be a one-time thing. All I knew was that I wanted more of Logan, and I hoped he wanted more of us.

Chapter 6

The summer was officially over. It had been over three months since Garrett and me had our first sexual encounter with Logan. However, that wasn't the one and only time we had sex with the pool boy. Far from it. After that first night we had sex, Logan came around more often and not just to clean and maintain our pool, but to hang out and spend the night with us too. He became our new best friend rather quickly. We went out to dinners, to the gay clubs, to the gym, and had many fun adventures and experiences with him.

I was beginning to see the many differences between Garrett and Logan the more we all hung out. And I had to admit to myself that what Garrett was lacking in, Logan made up for. Logan was always cool, calm, and collected. When any of us had a disagreement with each other, you could at least have an adult conversation with Logan about it. Garrett on the other hand would yell and go off the rails if no one agreed with him. Not only this, but there was just something that made Logan seem more humble than Garrett. And seeing a guy as hot as Logan show humility, made me absolutely wild about him.

But I think the best part about having Logan as a constant companion was that there were less frequent arguments between Garrett and me, to the point where the two of us stopped going to couple's therapy altogether. Maybe it was the fact that Logan elicited this new spark of energy between us that made everyone thrilled and excited, with no reason to have as many disagreements as we once had, or it could have been that Garrett and I would be completely embarrassed and ashamed to show this new catch, Logan, our flaws. After all, this was a whole new relationship for all of us. And during those first few months of bliss in a fresh romance, you always want to put on your best behavior and make yourself as extremely attractive as possible, while concealing anything negative about yourself. And that's exactly what we were doing now with Logan.

He was practically attached to our hip for the most part. Garrett and I absolutely loved having his company. Every time he did sleep over, he stayed in our bedroom, and slept right in between Garrett and me. Well, usually it turned into a long night of fucking, before we decided to actually fall asleep. Fucking Logan never got old. His body and face were out of this world and my physical attraction to him was permanent. My dick got hard at the mere sight of him.

Now don't get me wrong, there were a few early bumps in the road. For instance, after the first two months of all of us having our *friends with benefits* relationship, Logan announced that he had plans on going on a date with another man.

All three of us were at dinner together and he told us of this arrangement he made, halfway through the meal. "I hope you guys don't mind, but this guy, Austin, sort of asked me out on a date. I was hesitant at first...but then I said, 'why not?'" Logan confessed.

Garrett and I stared at each other blankly when he broke the news. It was a conversation the two of us never had before. Nor did we ever consider this idea. We were loving our current situation with Logan, being our fuck-buddy and always hanging out with us. I mean, he wasn't tied down to Garrett and me. Technically, he was still single. So, of course he could go out on a date with another guy if he wanted. That wouldn't be fair if Garrett and I prevented him from doing so. I made the only response to him that was appropriate. "That's great, Logan! I'm happy for you. I hope it works out," I said, hoping I sounded sincere enough.

But this was a complete lie. To be honest, I was extremely uneasy about Logan seeing another man. I suddenly felt knots in the pit of my stomach. It was aching, over me imagining the thought of someone else, besides me and Garrett, who was kissing him, feeling him, and worst of all, fucking him. I couldn't bear the thought.

Logan did his best to attempt to alleviate any worry we may have had. "Thanks. Yeah…it's a simple date. I doubt anything will come of it," he enthusiastically stated.

Garrett spoke up. "So, when is this date?"

Logan shrugged. "I'm guessing tomorrow night? We hadn't really made any firm plans. But I'm thinking then."

Garrett had a perplexed look on his face. "Hmmm? Well, whatever floats your boat, I guess," he said with annoyance. At least I was able to hide my emotions about how I felt about Logan seeing another person. Garrett, on the other hand, was doing a terrible job at it. Then again, Garrett always had a hard time concealing his thoughts and emotions from anyone, including myself.

The entire mood of the dinner changed after that. None of us were as lively as we typically were, and we didn't have much to say to one another. Logan's usual smile and jovial spirit diminished. He seemed very disheartened by Garrett's reaction, or maybe he felt slightly guilty about sharing this news with us. That was also a possibility.

I tried to start a new subject and keep everyone positive, but it didn't do much good. Logan and Garrett were both despondent. Things were even worse on the car ride home. No one had said a word to each other during the entire drive. As soon as we returned home, Logan made a suggestion. "I think I'm gonna head home tonight, if that's cool with you?"

The original plan was for Logan to stay the night again, but he was now having second thoughts, seeing how pissed Garrett was at him. Garrett didn't bother to turn around to face him while he spoke. "Whatever. Do what you gotta do."

I turned to Logan to see the dejected expression on his face. It took every ounce of control in my body to not go over and put my arms around him. I hated seeing him like this. However, I knew that if I did do that, Garrett would be beyond angry.

"Fine. I guess I'll see you around then," Logan said before he went upstairs to grab his bag of belongings. Now that he was upstairs, this gave Garrett and I some privacy together in the kitchen.

"Garrett, you don't have to be so hard on him. It's not his fault..." I began to say, but I was quickly interrupted by him.

"No, I get it. We're not exactly in a relationship with him, but still. I would have at least liked to have gotten a heads up about this, and not the day before he actually goes on a date with the guy," he explained.

"Well, let's be honest. You wouldn't have handled it well no matter what time he chose to tell us," I stated.

Garrett let out a deep grunt. "I hate it when you're right. I guess I can be a little more supportive."

I patted him on the back. "Atta boy!" I replied jokingly.

Logan came down the steps and was about to head straight out the door before Garrett called out to him. Logan stopped dead in his tracks and Garrett walked over to give him a long hug and kiss on the lips, before I came in to do the same with him. "Take care. Drive home safely," was all Garrett said.

This prompted Logan's smile to finally return. "Thanks! And I will. See you guys later."

He was out the door and gone. Garrett and I went into the living room and flopped down on the couch, turning on the television. Both of us were completely distracted and couldn't concentrate on the show that was on the screen. Our minds were completely consumed with thoughts of Logan Rippling. The thought of him being in a relationship with another man stressed the living hell out of us. We wanted him for ourselves, and we didn't want anyone else having him.

"I miss him already," Garrett whispered under his breath.

I decided to move closer to my husband on the couch and placed my arm around him. "I know. I feel the same," I added.

"Then why don't we do something about it, Scott?" He suggested.

"Well, what can we do? He's clear about going on a date with this Austin dude. I don't want to be the one to stop him," I mentioned.

"I know, but I wish we could let him know how we really feel. Maybe it might sway him in a different direction," Garrett thought out loud.

I shook my head. "Let him figure it out for himself. If he's really into us, he'll eventually come back. If not, then maybe it wasn't meant to be. I'd be sad to let him go, but we would get over it."

"I guess so," Garrett muttered.

For the rest of the night and the entire next day, Garrett and I were a complete wreck. The closer it came to the evening, when we assumed Logan would be going on his date, our panic and worry became more apparent.

"What if he winds up fucking him on the first date?"

"What if this Austin character is some serial killer?"

"If Logan does have sex, what happens if he gets an STD with this weirdo? He can't have sex with us ever again..."

"Do you think Logan will still be friends with us if he does have a boyfriend? Will he tell his boyfriend that we all had sex?"

"Will he stop talking to us altogether, after this? No. He wouldn't do that... would he?"

These were a few of the many questions Garrett and I exchanged with one another throughout the day.

It was going on eight o'clock now. We hadn't eaten all day, so we decided to get Chinese take-out. We were desperate for some comfort food that we could easily eat on our sofa. So, Chinese food seemed like the best option.

As we were halfway through our Lo Mein, we heard a loud knock at our door. Garrett and I were both caught off guard. "Who the hell could that be!?" He asked, perturbed by the inconvenience of having to get up to answer it.

Then, he and I both got out of our seats and went to the front door to open it. Much to our surprise, it was Logan. He was standing right in front of us, with his duffel bag in his hand. Logan dropped it to the ground the minute he saw us. He lunged forward to hug Garrett, before running over to grab and hug me as well.

He began to sob. "I couldn't do it. I just couldn't do it."

Garrett smiled at me before questioning him. "Couldn't do what?"

"Oh, come on, Garrett! You know what. I couldn't go on that date. I flaked on Austin and canceled on him at the last minute," Logan admitted.

I raised my brow to him, a little confused. "Why? Why didn't you go on the date with him?"

"Because...because of you two. I don't know how to explain it. It's so bizarre, but I think I *love* you. The both of you. And I don't want what we have to end. And me going on that date, I panicked and thought that it would ruin what we had," Logan confessed.

I squeezed him tighter in my arms. Garrett came from behind to hug him as well.

"Logan...we love you too. Scott and I weren't honest with you. We've been on an emotional roller coaster for the past day, thinking about you leaving us," Garrett revealed.

Logan's tears in his eyes started to disappear. "Really? Well, why didn't you guys tell me this ahead of time!?"

I shrugged. "I don't know. We were afraid you didn't feel the same way about us. But it's true, Logan. Garrett and I both love you…so much," I added.

The three of us stood there in the foyer, locked in a tight embrace with Logan sandwiched between us. "Well? Can we make this official, then?" Logan requested.

"Yeah. Let's do it. Just the three of us. We'll keep it closed and monogamous. Well, it would be polygamous…no wait…bigamous or trigamous?" I questioned the term out loud. Garrett and Logan both chuckled at my confusion.

"What he means is, yes, we'll be a *throuple.* We'll only have sex and be with each other. No one else," Garrett clarified.

We all agreed. To consummate this new defining moment in our relationship, the three of us headed upstairs, stripping our clothes down, along the way. Logan ran into the bedroom and jumped on the bed, spinning around to face us. As soon as I caught up to him, I spun him back around so that he was on his stomach. "Oh no you don't!" I growled.

"Damn! I love it when you're aggressive!" Logan growled back at me.

Garrett followed in suit and went to the opposite side of the bed so that he could force his cock down Logan's throat. I put my face down into Logan's ass.

The hottest fucking ass in the world that I couldn't get enough of!

After multiple position changes and the three of us cumming one right after the other, we laid down on the bed, facing the ceiling, just smiling and breathing heavily. Logan rested his head on my chest, and Garrett did as well.

Damn! How did I get so lucky? I had a hot husband and now a sexy, twink boyfriend. It couldn't get any better than this! Could it?

Logan traced his fingers up and down my torso as his other hand rubbed Garrett's back. "I love you, Garrett. I love you, Scott," he softly whispered.

My gaze shifted from the ceiling down to the back of his head that was laying on top of me. "Love you too, babe," I said.

Garrett echoed me. "Love you, sexy!"

So, it was official. We were in a throuple and on cloud nine right now. I never wanted this feeling and excitement to ever end. And at the rate our relationship was going, it seemed like this never would end. Would it? Only time would tell.

Chapter 7

"It's the most wonderful timeeeee of the yearrrrr."

The Christmas radio station played over the sound system in my office, as I was visiting my last patient in the screening room. "…so, I think you'll be fine, Mrs. Walden. I'm going to have my technician run some diagnostic tests to rule out all possibilities. We'll give you a call once we have the results. Otherwise, if everything looks good, which I imagine it will, then we'll keep you on a yearly follow-up appointment."

The frail old woman clasped her hands together. "Why thank you doctor! That is good news! What a Christmas miracle! I was so worried!" She exclaimed.

I smiled at her but was laughing on the inside at her rather dramatic gestures. I stood up and rubbed her shoulder gently as she sat in the patient's chair. "Have a wonderful holiday, Mrs. Walden."

She placed her fragile hand on top of mine. "You too, doctor! I hope you and your wife have a wonderful Christmas with your family!"

"That's the plan!" I said to her, before I released my hand from her shoulder and made my way out of the room. As much as I wanted to clarify to her that I had a husband, I didn't have it in me. Normally, I would have corrected someone for this assumption. However, this woman was old, and there was no point in trying to make her feel guilty about it. Maybe it was the holiday spirits that were also preventing me from doing so.

My cardiac technician, Cynthia, then came in to speak to Mrs. Walden, before running her tests.

That was it. My last patient of the day. I was officially off for a much needed Christmas vacation. Cynthia was already planning to help finish up some of the charts for the evening. She begged me to go ahead and leave once I was finished with Mrs. Walden. She assured me that she would close and lock up. I was hesitant at first, but finally agreed to leave.

Garrett and Logan were home waiting for me. Logan still wasn't technically living under our roof, but he was still over our place nearly every day of the week. It was Christmas Eve, and we had plans on eating a nice dinner together, over a few bottles of expensive wine. We would exchange gifts with one another and end the night with some hot, steamy sex. Tonight though, we were doing things a bit differently. Instead of fucking in the bedroom as we normally did, we would be laying a blanket out on the living room floor by the fireplace, feeling the warmth of both the embers and each other's bodies.

As I got home, I took my coat and shoes off, putting them in the coat closet. I could smell the aroma of something delicious. I walked into the kitchen to see Logan in an apron and a chef hat. Except, that was all! No really, that's all he wore. As I moved around the kitchen island to get a full visual of him, he was bare naked, in merely that white apron and a white chef hat.

Mmmmm! What a sexy little fucker!

I came up behind him and wrapped my hands around his waist, with my cock pressed against my dress pants and into the crevice of his smooth, bare ass. I tilted my head to softly kiss and nibble on his neck.

"Is it time for dessert yet?" I pleaded.

Logan leaned forward to prevent me from kissing him any longer. "No! It's not!" He laughed with me and spun around to make out with me.

Garrett entered the room and came up to us, smacking Logan on the ass. "I warned him it was a bad idea to wear this. I told him we wouldn't even make it to dinner." Garrett leaned forward to kiss me on the lips. "Welcome home, babe. Merry Christmas Eve," he said to me.

"Thanks, Gare. Merry Christmas Eve!" I replied to him.

I had to admit, ever since Logan came along, mine and Garrett's relationship seemed almost repaired. We barely fought or argued anymore, and Garrett was always in a good mood and had a positive attitude except on some minor occasions. We were always in high-spirits and most importantly (at least it was the most important to *me*) our sex life was the best it has been in years. Yes, we only had sex now when we were with Logan, but still, it counted. During our three-ways, there have been times when I fucked Garrett and even Logan fucked him too. I would say out of the three of us, I mostly topped, followed by Garrett, who has been fairly versatile for the most part. Meanwhile, Logan tended to bottom almost all the time, but when he was really in the mood, he topped Garrett. Although I think Logan considers himself versatile, he mostly bottoms for us.

What can I say? He was so goddamn fuckable! I only wanted him to bottom and nothing else!

I tapped Logan on the ass and stepped away to give him some personal space. This allowed him to chop up some vegetables. I finally took the time to get a good view of everything he had laid out on the countertops. "So, what exactly are you cooking us tonight?" I asked.

I was very intrigued. A few months ago, Logan had requested that he cook for Garrett and me. Usually, the three of us would always go out to dine or have food delivered to the house. Even before Logan came into our lives, this was a common pattern Garrett and I continued. So, when Logan made us this elaborate dinner of chicken cacciatore, rosemary roasted potatoes, garlic bread, and quinoa for the first time, a few months ago, I was completely taken aback.

Logan kept surprising us with his hidden talents. Since that night, he cooked for all of us at least once or twice a week. He insisted upon it. Garrett and I couldn't argue against it. Besides, everything he had cooked or baked for us since then had been absolutely delicious!

Logan moved over to the oven to turn on the light in it, checking on whatever was cooking inside, which gave me the perfect view of that gorgeous, bubble butt of his. He turned back around to face us. "I have a baked ham in the oven with some brown sugar glaze. Then, we have some cranberry brie bites and spinach artichoke zucchini bites you all can munch on for now, if you want, until everything else is ready. The roasted brussels sprouts and roasted red potatoes should also be done any minute. But once the brussels sprouts and potatoes are done in the bottom oven, I need to heat up the honey-garlic cauliflower for a bit."

Jesus! How many people was he cooking for!? This was a lot!

"Damn, babe! You really outdid yourself!" I exclaimed, as I snatched one of the cranberry brie bites he had offered. Garrett did the same.

"Well, it is Christmas Eve after all! So, I wanna make sure we have a really nice dinner together, before we have to see our families, separately, tomorrow," he explained.

Garrett wrapped his arms around Logan's waist. "Well it all looks phenomenal, babe!" He commented to Logan.

We decided to spend Christmas Eve with one another and exchange gifts tonight. During Christmas Day, Garrett and I had two families to visit. We went to my parents' house in the morning to be with my family, before we travelled to Garrett's aunt and uncle's house for the evening, to be with his family. No one in our family knows about Logan, so it would be extremely awkward for us to bring him around during the holidays. We would inevitably be bombarded with questions and suspicions about him, which I was definitely trying to avoid.

But the good thing was that Logan also did his own thing with his family on Christmas Day too. So, for this year, at least, we were all squared away. And who knows how next year would turn out. Hell, I wasn't sure if we would have the bravery to let anyone in our families know that we were all in a throuple, even by then.

Suddenly, Logan pulled off his apron so that he was now completely naked.

Woah! Was he ready to get fucked right here, right now, on the kitchen countertop!?

I mean, I was ready to give it to him if he wanted, but he expelled that thought right out the window. "I'm gonna go upstairs and change into something more suitable for dinner. Do one of you mind pulling the potatoes and brussels sprouts out of the oven in five minutes and putting the honey-garlic cauliflower in? I should be back downstairs in time before the ham is ready."

"Sure. We'll take care of it," I said. As Logan tried to move past us for the stairs, Garrett and I both smacked his ass hard. Did he really think he was going to get by us without getting touched in some shape or form? He gave a loud yelp once he felt the smacks. "Owww! You little fuckers! That's probably going to leave a mark!" He snickered while yelling this out loud.

Garrett and I busted out in laughter at Logan's over the top reaction. "That was the intent! Now get that ass of yours upstairs, before we give you seconds!" Garrett yelled to him.

Logan gave us both the middle finger and sprinted upstairs so that neither one of us could catch him in time.

"Little shit. He's lucky he's so damn cute," I jokingly stated to Garrett.

He shrugged. "We'll get him back later. He forgets that we have the blankets laid out across the living room floor, all ready for tonight. He won't be going anywhere when we tie him down."

I walked over to the kitchen bar and popped open a bottle of the Chateau Garraud Lalande de Pomerol, an expensive Bordeaux we usually drank on special occasions, such as this. I pulled three wine glasses down from the cabinet and gave a generous pour in each of them. I glanced over to see that Garrett was taking care of Logan's oven request. I carried Logan's and Garrett's glasses of wine to the kitchen island, before returning to grab my own.

Garrett and I chatted before Logan came back downstairs, having changed into a tight dark blue sweater and tan khakis.

That boy could even make torn rags look good on him!

I handed his red wine glass to him. The three of us stood side by side. Garrett raised his glass in the air, expecting us to do the same. "Here's to our first of many Christmases together! Cheers!" We clinked our glasses, hearing the sound echo and permeate through every room in the house. I don't think we could ever have a glass of wine without Garrett needing to make a toast. But it was always a nice, thankful gesture on his part, which I did appreciate.

We finally ate dinner and exchanged gifts by the Christmas Tree in the living room. Logan got Garrett and me a few pairs of clothes, but nothing overly extravagant, which is understandable, based on him being a college student, without a full-time job. I didn't expect him to go out of his way to make a heavy purchase on us. But what I was stunned by was what Garrett had given Logan, which was an expensive Bremont watch. It had a sapphire face with diamond studs on the outskirts of it. It had to have been well over a thousand dollars.

However, I had the same thought process as Garrett, and also surprised Logan with my own special gift, unbeknownst to Garrett. It was a platinum bracelet with bright diamonds embedded along the entire length of it. Garrett raised a brow when he saw the surprise gift, I had given Logan He obviously had no remark to make over it. After all, he did the same thing. It would be completely hypocritical if he did make a fuss about it.

As soon as we were done with our gift exchange, we wasted no time in getting down on the floor on the red satin blankets and sheets. The fire was ablaze, and our wine glasses were full, once again. We placed them on the hearth of the fireplace, right next to the lube.

Of course, someone just happened to have strategically placed that bottle there.

Logan was the first to lay sprawled out, across the sheets. I motioned to lean over top of Logan and gave him a long, soft kiss on the lips. "Thank you for dinner and the gifts, babe. They were really thoughtful," I whispered to him.

Logan returned the kiss. "Of course. Thank you, as well." He rolled over out from under me to get closer to Garrett to give him the same lingering kiss he had given me. "And thank you too, sexy," he addressed Garrett.

Once they separated from one another, Garrett came over to kiss me, while placing his hand behind Logan's head, pressing him in, to make out with the both of us. All three of us elicited our passion with one another. The scene of the lit fireplace, the Christmas Tree lights glowing, us laying across the red satin sheets, with glasses of red wine, evoked a sensual ambiance.

This scene we had created wasn't meant for fucking. It was meant for pure, passionate, love-making. Foreplay was on the rise. I traced my hands all across Logan's cheeks and neck, taking the time to feel the warmth of his skin. Logan leaned his face into my hands to let me feel him. Garrett already had his shirt off and grabbed Logan's hand, pressing it against his chest, wanting Logan to feel every inch of his thick pec muscles. We went back to kissing one another. Almost intricately, we each pulled our shirts and pants off, not daring to try and separate our lips from each other, unless forced to, for the quick second to get our shirts over our heads.

I looked down and was very surprised at what I saw. Logan was wearing a tight, silky red and white Christmas thong. "And what do we have here?" I pointed to it.

Logan tried his best to look as innocent as possible, but it wasn't working all too well for him.

Garrett chimed in. "I guess this is an extra Christmas gift?"

Logan nodded. "Something like that," he whimpered. "Now get your ass down here!" Logan pulled Garrett down into him.

I watched as Logan raised his bent legs into the air, while lying on his back. Garrett was now on top of him, kissing his lips. His hands were spread wide, moving up and down Logan's side and thick quad muscles. I too moved my hands to feel Logan's body. I managed to dig my hands into the front of his thong to grab his fully hardened cock. He moaned at the sudden touch. I began stroking it, while Garrett continued to tie his tongue with Logan's.

Garrett leaned back and started pulling Logan's thong off, forcing me to release my hand from his dick. Garrett and I both then proceeded to pull off our underwear, as well. We were all now fully stripped down, and hard.

I moved forward to have myself on top of Logan. Our cocks massaged one another, as I slowly humped him, tasting his tongue with mine. His hands wrapped around to my back and dug deep into it. Out of the corner of my eye, I could see Garrett was pulling something out, from underneath the sheets. Logan opened his eyes and saw this as well. We both pulled away from one another, interested in what Garrett was up to.

Garrett held out a black dress tie. "Let's play a little game. Shall we?" He wrapped the tie around Logan's head and made sure the thick end of the tie was towards the front. He knotted it so that Logan was now fully blindfolded.

Oh! I totally wanted to play this game, where everyone was a winner!

Logan smiled, not knowing what to expect. "What are you gonna do to me?"

Garrett placed his index finger over Logan's lips. "Shhhh. Just feel…" Garrett slowly pressed that same finger into Logan's mouth. I could see Logan was massaging Garrett's finger with his tongue as he slowly sucked on it. Garrett pulled it out and stood up, walking out of the room and into the kitchen.

To bide the time, I moved my hands across Logan's chest, slowly tracing my fingers around his nipples, before squeezing them softly. "Mmmmm," he moaned in pleasure as I did this, confirming that he was enjoying it.

I turned my head while doing so, to see Garrett walking back into the room, with a number of items in his arms. The first was a cup, that looked like it had some sticky brown substance in it. When brought it closer to me, I could smell that it was hot fudge. He also held a Ziploc bag of ice cubes and placed a lit candle from the kitchen on the hearth, along with the other objects.

"Alright, Logan, are you ready to *feel?*" Garrett asked seductively.

"Yes…I'm ready." Logan gulped. I could notice the sweat on Logan's neck. It glimmered as the lit fire reflected off it. The way Logan looked now had me fully entranced with him. He was innocent, submissive, and forced to handle whatever we gave him. It fucking turned me on so much.

Garrett grabbed the candle from its holder and held it over Logan. The wax slowly dripped from it. It flowed from Logan's chest all the way down to his navel. "Ahhhh…" Logan softly whimpered, feeling the intensity of the heat traveling down his body.

This time, I placed my index finger over his mouth as he made this noise. I leaned over to whisper in his ear. "Shhhh. Again…just *feel*." He lightly bit it at first, before he sucked on it.

Garrett put the candle back in the holder and reached for the bag of ice. He pulled out a cube from it and held it in his hand. He placed the ice cube over Logan's chest and ran it down the same trail that the wax made. Logan instantly shivered once he felt it. "Holy fuck!" He blurted out.

I jammed my finger further into his mouth to keep him quiet. He continued to moan and lightly gagged as soon as I did this. He returned to sucking on it once again.

Garrett took the ice cube on a longer journey, further than the melted wax. I saw him trace the ice around Logan's cock. He lifted Logan's leg in the air and nodded at the other one, wanting me to lift his other leg up too, which I did. Now that Logan's legs and feet were both in the air, Garrett used his other hand to continue to run the ice cube down to Logan's taint, holding it there for a brief moment. He began to rub it up and down.

Logan squirmed, feeling the sensitivity of the chill from the ice. Garrett continued to tactfully toy with Logan. The ice was now melting, and its cold drips ran down Logan's crack and towards his hole.

This was so fucking sensuous!

I did my best to not stick my tongue in it to lick it off. Garrett then allowed the ice cube to reach its final destination, which was at Logan's asshole. With what remained of the ice, Garrett rubbed the cube against it, slowly before plunging it into Logan's hole along with two of his fingers.

Logan screamed out in ecstasy. "Mmmmmm!!! Fuckkkk!" He rolled his hips from side to side as if he wanted Garrett's fingers to go deeper.

Logan's hole was hungry, and he wanted more. And soon enough, he would be getting more. All of me in that fucking sweet boy-hole of his.

I decided to grab the bottle of lube and soak my dick with it. Garrett gave me an odd look as I did this, unsure of what I was planning on doing while he had his fingers still inside Logan. I moved in front of Logan so that my cock was ready and aimed to dive right into that amazing, tight hole of his.

I grabbed Garrett's hand with my wrist and gently pulled it so that his fingers were coming out of Logan. The instant they were out, I substituted my cock in their place and pushed it in, gradually. This made Logan lose all control. He knew exactly what was happening. "Holy shit!!! Oh my god! Fuck me! Please, fuck me! I can't take it anymore! Pleaseeee!!!" He begged.

I did as he requested. I grunted heavily, feeling those ass muscles wrap around my cock and I thrusted in and out of him. As I fucked Logan, I watched Garrett out of the corner of my eye, grabbing a small vial from the side. It was a bottle of poppers we rarely used. After all, there was no need for Garrett or me to ever have to sniff them. Garrett was more than capable of taking my cock without needing to use muscle relaxers in order to do so. Plus, those chemicals from the poppers weren't exactly helping Garrett's AFib. So, I wondered why he was pulling them out now. But he soon made his intentions crystal clear.

"You're going to take *both* of us, Logan. I want you to take mine and Scott's dick up your hole at the same time. Got it?" Garrett spoke in such a low, demonic tone, with an edge of sexiness behind it.

I was stunned by Logan's immediate nod, without any reluctance. Garrett opened up the bottle and held it to Logan's nose. He pushed his finger against the outside of one of Logan's nostrils, shutting it. "Sniff," he demanded. Logan did so, before sniffing the inhalant with the other nostril too. I stopped pounding Logan, but kept my hard cock inside him, still. I was curious to see how Garrett intended on positioning himself, so that we both could have access to Logan's ass.

Garrett moved so that he was under Logan. He lifted Logan up and scooted himself beneath him. It forced me to have to pull out of Logan for the moment. Slowly, Garrett inserted his erection into Logan. Both Logan and Garrett were now on their backs, facing me, except that Logan was on top of Garrett. "Come on, Scott. Your turn," Garrett stated.

"Mhmm. I can take it, Scott. Go for it," Logan assured me. So, I pushed myself into him, right above Garrett's cock.

Logan screamed at first, causing me to slow down. But my dick still managed to slip further into him, with more ease than I had anticipated. It was so fucking tight, and the added pressure of feeling Garrett's cock move up and down against mine, providing it added friction, felt like nothing I've ever experienced before in my entire life.

I couldn't believe what I was witnessing. We were now double-penetrating Logan and he was taking both of us without any issues. So, I picked up my pace with thrusting into him. I tried to go opposite to Garrett's rhythm. When he slid in, I slid out. When he moved out, I pushed in. It was so intense. But Logan's pain was becoming more evident. The expression on his face told me he wasn't enjoying it as much as I had thought. He was tolerating more pain than experiencing pleasure. I didn't like to see him afflicted in this way, causing me to pull out of him. Garrett did the same, giving Logan a sense of relief and a moment to breathe. But I could tell Logan still wanted to more. And we weren't through with him yet.

Garrett grabbed the cup of hot fudge and started rubbing it all on his shaft and tip. He kneeled and traced his thumb along Logan's lips, signaling for him to open his mouth. The second he did, Garrett pressed his cock right into Logan's mouth, allowing Logan to taste his chocolate-soaked dick. Logan was able to make one quick comment. "Mmmmm. That's fucking good!" Then, Garrett pressed himself further into Logan's throat, preventing him from uttering a single word. Logan couldn't help but uncontrollably squirm. He tried to reach around to grab his own dick with his hand. I pressed his wrist down into the sheets, blocking him from doing so. "No! Just fucking feel!" I commanded him. My strokes in and out of his ass soon intensified. Logan kept trying to shift and jerk around, but my and Garrett's weight on top of him stopped him from moving too much.

All he did was groan and then…I couldn't believe what happened. My eyes widened and so did Garrett's, as Logan shook his hips up and down. I saw the white liquid shoot across his stomach in a puddle.

Logan just fucking jizzed, without even touching himself…without anyone touching him!

This was a first for me. I had never seen anyone shoot their load without their dick being stroked. It was enough to make me bust all inside of him too.

"Fuck! Fuckkkkkk!!!!" I yelled as my thrusts slowed their pace, but I continued to push in, as deep as I could, wanting every last ounce of my cum inside him.

Garrett closed his eyes and wrapped his hand around Logan's head. "Just like that baby…keep that mouth on it just like that. Don't stop… Don't stop. Here it comes…Just like that. Fuckkkkk!" Garrett groaned, fully pumping himself down Logan's throat.

The two of us pulled out of both of Logan's holes and knelt over him. Finally, Logan had his hands released and went to lift the tie from his face. His alluring blue-green eyes were then revealed, staring up at Garrett and me in wonder.

"That…was…incredible!" He managed to say, while he panted heavily, gasping for breath in between each word. "I…have never… experienced…anything…like that," he finished off saying.

Garrett and I had a bright smile, showing across our faces. We laid down and turned Logan's face towards each of us to kiss him.

"Glad you enjoyed it," Garrett replied. "We all actually enjoyed it, of course," he added.

"I did enjoy it…a lot. I love you two," Logan whispered.

I planted another kiss on his lips. "Love you too, Logan," I said.

Garrett parroted me. "Love you too."

As we laid down, we reflected on one of, if not *the*, best sexual experiences we've ever had in our entire lives.

Then, I was reminded of something I had forgotten. "Oh! I'll be right back."

"Where are you going?" Logan asked me.

"Give me one second," I requested, before I stood up and walked into my office to grab a small, wrapped box in the back of the drawer. I brought it back to the guys and sat down beside them with it in my hands.

"What's that?" Logan inquired.

"One final surprise we had planned," Garrett answered.

"Go ahead and open it," I suggested.

I handed the small gift to Logan and he unwrapped it, revealing a tiny white box. As soon as he opened it, his face lit up, like fireworks in the night sky.

"It's a key!?" He exclaimed.

"Yeah. A key to our house," Garrett clarified.

I further explained its significance. "Logan, you are so special to us. Garrett and I have been talking and we want you to officially move in."

Logan displayed a quizzical expression on his face. "But don't I already live here? I'm practically here seven days a week."

"Yeah…but we were hoping you would end the rental on your apartment and literally move in here with us. You could change your address and bring your entire wardrobe and whatever else you need here as well," Garrett stated.

Logan leaned in to hug the both of us. "Of course, I will! I wouldn't dream of living anywhere else!" He proclaimed.

Garrett grabbed his glass of wine and held it out, waiting for us to follow his lead.

Here comes one of Garrett's toasts, yet again.

"Here's to another big step in our relationship and many more surprises to come!" We tapped our glasses together with his.

Garrett was completely accurate in his statement. There were many more surprises to come in our relationship. Many, many more.

Chapter 8

"We need to talk," Garrett privately said to me when Logan was out running an errand. It had been three months since Logan officially moved into our home.

"Sure, what about?" I asked him. There was something odd going on with Garrett. I could sense his most recent happy-go-lucky attitude start to digress. There was a shift in the way he handled situations. His impatience was incrementally growing, and he would start to argue with Logan and me over the smallest of things. It was déjà vu all over again. I hoped this was merely a phase and that the old Garrett, who raised hell, would not be making a permanent appearance back into our lives.

"It's about Logan," Garrett revealed. "And about us. The only time us two ever have sex is with Logan, and I notice that we are always touching Logan, but we rarely give attention to each other, anymore."

I shook my head. "I don't think that at all. If anything, I think Logan has made our sex life and physical attraction to one another stronger. Even when we are in bed with him, I'm constantly rubbing on you and showing you affection."

"Really? Is that what you think?" Garrett asked, as if he was looking for some sort of additional verification.

"Of course! Don't you?"

"No. I'm beginning to wonder if Logan is simply the glue that's holding us together. I don't know. It just seems like each of our own relationships with him is blossoming, but the relationship between the two of us remains stagnant. Yes, we are arguing a lot less, and all, but have things really improved? What if Logan upped and left us today? Would you and I still be okay, or would things go back to the way they once were, like when we were in counseling?" Garrett questioned.

"Look, Garrett. I think you're overthinking things right now. Honestly, anyone of us can leave this relationship at any point. You can't predict what the future holds, but I hope that it includes all three of us, and that's what you should hope for too. Try not to think about the hypotheticals. Just live life each day and appreciate and cherish the time that we all have together. I've seen so many patients with horror stories of early deaths in their families and relationships, yet here we are, having double the love in ours. Do you get what I'm saying?"

"I suppose so," Garrett stated, with a heavy sigh behind it. "I hope things continue the way they are going. I wouldn't want us to go back to the way they once were, with us having so many problems."

Garrett must have been a self-fulfilling prophet, because that is exactly what happened in the following year. All of our turmoil and any fights we had were all because of Garrett and his insecurities.

"You two are always ganging up on me!"

"Both of you are giving each other more attention during sex and leaving me alone."

"Logan always agrees with you! He's always taking your side!"

"You both wouldn't care if I died. You would go on living your life together, not giving a fuck about me."

Garrett would throw these terrible comments around more frequently, as time went on. But the truth was that now I was the one becoming more and more impatient with the way he was acting. Garrett was always like this, but now that Logan was in the picture and I could see that there was someone I could compare Garrett to, Logan was glowing brighter and brighter, every day to me.

The year flew by. It was already the following summer. Logan, Garrett, and I had already taken two vacations together. The first was a Spring cruise in the Caribbean. The second, was a week-long trip to Greece. We stayed in Mykonos at the Elysium Hotel. There were hot, muscular, tan man at every turn. In the hotel, bars, clubs, on the beach, by the pool, practically everywhere. All three of us took notice at some of these sexy Herculean gods that were around us. However, none of them held a candle to Logan.

There were times where I found myself a little jealous of the crazy amount of stares Logan received. Some of the men had the nerve to grab Logan by the ass and chest as they passed by him. I'm usually not an insecure man, but when it came to Logan, I was beyond protective and admittedly jealous at times, when I saw giant, colossal men hitting on him. This was something I eventually had gotten used to. I mean, just look at Logan. Even if I were single and didn't know him, I would be tempted to get my hands on him too, even if it was for a brief second.

However, Garrett was a pain in the ass to deal with, during our vacations. He complained over the most ridiculous of things, including the service at the restaurants, the times we decided we wanted to lay out on the beaches, where exactly we wanted to go out to dinner, and so much more. He always found a way to either victimize himself and claim that Logan and I were ganging up on him, or he would try to disagree with us for the fuck of it.

Although my relationship with Logan was strong and the passion was still there, my relationship with Garrett was once again taking a turn for the worse, over the past few months. Garrett was returning to his old ways. He would raise his voice and start arguing with me over the craziest things. He was making mountains out of mole-hills. There were even times when he got nasty with Logan, which was the worst.

I was fine with him taking his anger out on me, but when he did it to Logan, who did absolutely nothing wrong to him, I became pissed. Today was our most heated argument.

"So, you two are going to work together now, leaving me hung out to dry!?" Garrett yelled.

I shook my head. "For Christ's sake, Garrett! Logan needs some work experience. He is going into his senior year in Human Services. Nowhere else will give him a paid position, unless he's graduated. They are only looking for interns. How many times do we have to go over this?" I asked.

Logan silently sat on the sofa, which he typically did whenever Garrett was having one of his tantrums. "That's bullshit, Scott! You have tons of connections. You could easily get him a job anywhere. He doesn't have to work with you as your front office manager," Garrett explained.

"I still don't see what the big deal is, Garrett. I asked you to work in my practice for the past two years and you've turned it down every single time. I'm not sure why you care," I replied to him.

Garrett slapped his palm to his forehead. "You still don't get it!? This has been going on for the past few months. You and Logan are getting closer and closer, while you and I are growing apart!" He admitted.

"Garrett, are you being serious right now!? I give you as much attention as I do him," I defended myself. I turned to look at Logan who still sat there, quietly. I felt awful that he had to listen to this ridiculousness. Garrett's absurdities were in a league of their own.

"No, you don't, Scott! You don't touch me the way you touch him. You don't look at me the way you look at him. And now, he's going to work every day with you too!? I can't believe you didn't think this would be a problem!" Garrett exclaimed.

He bolted out of the room before we could finish the argument.

"Where are you going now!?" I yelled to him. I walked into the kitchen to see where he was headed.

"Out. Don't bother calling me. I won't be home until later tonight. I need to vent," he scowled. Garrett headed right out the door. Soon enough, I heard the car engine start up and the garage door open. I peered out through the front window to see him driving away.

I returned to the family room to Logan. "I swear! It's always something with him!" I expressed in annoyance.

I sat on the sofa beside him, placing my elbows on my knees, holding my head in my hands. It was frustrating as hell when Garrett got like this. It was like there was a quick switch in his head that had an "on" and "off" button. Nothing in between.

I suddenly felt a soothing, circular motion on my back. I glanced up to see Logan had scooted closer to me on the couch and was now rubbing me.

"I'm sorry, Scott. It's not your fault. Really, it's mine," he spoke in a downtrodden manner.

I placed my hand on his inner thigh and squeezed it. "No, Logan. It's not your fault. This is not your fault by any means. I'm sorry that you have to deal with it. It's one thing for me to have put up with it for years, but it's another thing to have dragged you into it. And now, you have to tolerate it too," I replied.

"I don't mind tolerating it…I really don't." He smiled endearingly.

"And that's why I love you, Logan. You are completely unselfish, thoughtful, caring, and sexy as hell, of course. You're everything. You shouldn't have to put up with this bullshit," I told him. I met his gaze with my own, staring deeply into those oceanic eyes of his, with my hand now holding his cheek.

"No. I know I don't have to put up with it. But I do it all for you, Scott. I am madly in love with you. I can't lie to myself. If you left this relationship, I don't think Garrett and I would last very long together. But if it were only you and me, I would still be head over heels. I still feel that way about you to this day and always have, ever since we first got together," he confessed.

It was as if my emotions were small chemicals in all different parts of my body. As soon as Logan revealed this to me, all of those chemicals came together into one giant combustion of reactions and fireworks.

I grabbed his face with my hands and brought my head into his, kissing him on the lips. I closed my eyes, allowing myself to get lost in him. Logan wrapped one of his hands around to the back of my head, lightly tugging on my hair while he made out with me.

My hands started to have a mind of their own as they moved down to his side. I placed them under his shirt, so I could grab his obliques. He too reached under my clothes, except I could feel his delicate fingers trickle across my chest and stomach as our lips remained inseparable.

This was one of the first times Logan and I had the entire house alone to ourselves. Deep down, I knew it would be a bad idea to have sex with him and without Garrett. Logan and I never had sex with one another without Garrett present. However, that never meant that the idea had never crossed my mind. I thought about it all too often, since the first time we ever did have sex. What I would do to fuck Logan Rippling alone, to give him all of my attention. He would be forced to have no other distractions, besides me. He would experience all of me, fully devoted to him, and nothing else. I wanted this badly.

So, as much as I wanted to keep my promise to Garrett about not fucking Logan without him, it was hard to, in this moment. The way he had been acting these past several months was making me feel less guilty about breaking it. Plus, he would be out of the house for a while. What if I did fuck Logan alone? He wouldn't have to know about it.

I realized I was trying to find every excuse I could gather, to reason with myself on why I should fuck Logan. And those reasons now had me sold.

Fuck it all! I'm going for it!

I abruptly pulled away from kissing Logan and stood up, holding my hand out to him. He gave me a devilish grin and winked, accepting my hand. I led him upstairs and into the bedroom, practically dragging him the whole way. I released his hand forward, with force, so that he went flopping ahead of me, onto the bed. I crawled right on top of him, kissing him once again. My hands found his hands that were now stretched out, high above his head. As our hands met, our fingers locked and intertwined as we continued to taste each other.

I could see that Logan didn't seem to care that we were breaking our promise to Garrett, which I too found understandable based on Garrett's shitty behavior.

Fuck Garrett! Enough about him!

I detached all thoughts about Garrett. Logan was my only focus in this very moment. He was my only carnal desire, and I was his. We pulled each other's clothes off as fast as we could. I began breathing deeply, seeing Logan's fully toned body on display. It was all mine and belonged to no one else.

He rested his head down on the pillow, gazing up at me with that sexy, innocent expression he often gave that melted me, every time. One of his arms moved behind his head to pose for me, while his other arm reached out to me. He placed his hand on my kneecap. Logan slowly moved it up my leg until it met my cock that was now fully erect.

I let out a light gasp when he began to move his clenched hand up and down on it. I closed my eyes for only a split second, and when I opened them, my light gasp turned into a loud one. Logan's face was on my dick. From my point of view, I could see the top of his head bobbing. I gave a subtle shiver at the intensity I was experiencing from his warm, wet mouth.

He started to pick up the pace. His mouth was like a fucking vacuum. As he did this, he opened his eyes and tilted his head slightly upward, continuing to blow me. He kept making eye contact with me as my cock owned his mouth.

He knew what he was doing. It was my greatest weakness. My biggest turn on during a blow job was when Logan glared up at me with his eyes wide open, savagely sucking me off. I had to immediately grab him by the head and push his face off me. He was so close to making me cum, but there was no way I was going to simply ejaculate in his mouth and be done.

Absolutely no fucking way!

I wasn't going to waste this opportunity with having Logan alone, to finish with strictly a blow job. Fuck no! He was going to take my dick up his ass, and he would be moaning and begging me for it. He would be desperate for *me*, wanting no one else. Only *me*.

Logan rolled across the bed and reached into the nightstand for the lube. He prepped his hole with it, before pouring it onto my dick. He rubbed it all over for me. Logan turned around so he was now on his stomach. He hunched up, so that all of his weight was now on his knees. Leaning further forward, he arched his back into the perfect "C" while he was on all fours. He wanted it doggy-style and that's how he was going to get it.

I positioned myself right behind him, holding my dick. I inserted the tip and let it rest, barely inside his hole. He moaned and turned his head around so he could see me out of the corner of his eye. He was probably wondering why I wasn't pumping the full length of my shaft into him and fucking his brains out, by now.

"Come on, daddy. Fucking give it to me. Please…" he seductively whispered to me.

That's what I was waiting for.

I wanted him begging for my dick. Begging for me to pleasure him. I pressed forward, while squeezing his sides as hard as possible. Logan let out a heavy yell before pressing his face down into the pillow.

"Fuck yeah, boy. That's it. Take daddy's dick! You can handle it. Come on!" I howled in a deep voice.

I could see his feet starting to flex, with his toes curling, as I increased my rhythm. "I can't get enough of that thick, fucking cock!" He loudly admitted.

I reached my hand forward to pull his hair, yanking him back up in the air so his face was now forward, and not down into the pillow. "What was that you said!? I couldn't fucking hear you…" I trailed off as I continued to fuck Logan mercilessly.

"Fuck me, daddy! Fuck my hole deeper! I want you balls deep in me!"

I loved this side of Logan! He never sounded this verbally dirty when Garrett and I were fucking him together. Here, he was being his authentic self and letting his true sexual urges run wild, and it was *me* bringing this out in him. I was loving every second of it.

I completely pulled out of him, suddenly, and I could see his asshole clench tight when he flopped down, flat into the bed. His hole continued to pulsate, as if it was missing and longing for my cock. His ass knew my dick belonged in it.

Logan turned around with a wild expression of confusion on his face. "Why did you pull out!?" He demanded to know.

"I want to see that face of yours when I cum. I want to see the look on your face as you squirm, knowing I'm breeding you raw!" I exclaimed.

Fuck. I was losing complete control of myself!

I was never usually this verbal or aggressive in bed. Logan must have brought this out in me as well.

On cue, he turned around on his back, with his head on the pillow. I wrapped my hands around his ankles and lifted his legs in the air. I inched forward and let his calves rest on my shoulders. Now that I had him balanced and right where I wanted him, I pressed my thumb down on the top of my erect dick and guided it, directly into his hot, slippery hole.

He closed and scrunched his eyes, feeling me fully immersed in him, once again. I cupped my hands on his shoulders and pushed my body down towards Logan, so my cock could reach its greatest length inside him.

"Mmmmm," he whimpered, reaching for his own dick, now stroking it. I pounded him as he did this. My dick was throbbing around his ass muscles that squeezed tightly around it.

"Open your eyes..." I softly said, before my tone became more assertive. "Open those fucking eyes! I want to look into those fucking eyes when I cum in you!" I commanded.

"Fuck, Scott! You're gonna make me shoot, babe!" He managed to get this out, in between his moans.

I was on the verge of releasing my load into him. I placed my hand over his throat and squeezed it, giving it a moderate choke. Logan's eyes bulged as I did this, and he loved every second of it.

"Fuck daddy! Right there! Oh my god, I can't hold it any... Arghhhh!!!!" Logan screamed, shooting his white cum out, like a fucking geyser. It busted straight up his chest, partially across his cheek, and behind his head, onto the backboard of the bed.

The entire scene was enough to push me to my breaking point. I pressed down harder on his throat, as I was now ejaculating into him. "Yeah baby! Take it all! Take every fucking bit of it!" I continued thrusting into him as I came.

I didn't have the energy to pull my cock out from him. I just collapsed right on top of Logan. My face was right next to his, buried into the pillow. I could feel his hand on the back of my head holding me as we both panted.

"And what the fuck is this!? Are you fucking kidding me!? I knew it!!! You fucking liars!!!"

I turned my head around to see where the irate shouting was coming from.

There was a sinking feeling in my stomach when I saw that it was Garrett, standing in the doorway of our bedroom, staring at us in bewilderment.

Chapter 9

That night, things were extremely intense. Garrett had caught Logan and me having sex without him. We had broken the promise we made together, that we would never fuck when one of us was away. Garrett clearly had zero trust in us now and I didn't blame him.

However, I didn't blame Logan and I either. Garrett's shitty attitude was the main reason for it all. Him acting this way for the past several months was what really pushed Logan and I closer together and made us want to have sex without him. Garrett was emotionally isolating himself from us and I was surprised that he was not able to recognize that.

Not only did Garrett yell at me when we were caught, but he also let Logan have it. "And you…I don't know who the fuck you think you are! I brought you into this relationship, and I could easily push you right out of it! So, don't fucking try me!" He threatened Logan.

Logan moved closer to Garrett to try and appease him, by grabbing his hand, but Garrett wasn't having any of it. He withdrew his hand hard and fast from Logan. "Don't fucking touch me! You filthy fucking slut!" He shouted. "I'm done with this shit. I'm sleeping in the guest room tonight. You two can continue to fuck each other like monkeys, all you want now, since I won't be in bed with you tonight. That's what you really wanted all along, right!?" He accused us.

I spoke up. "Garrett, we can have a civil conversation about this. But I'm not going to bother with it, if you're just going to stand here with the yelling and name-calling," I told him.

"Oh, that's rich, coming from you! Whatever..." As Garrett said this, he walked into one of the guest bedrooms, down the hall, and slammed the door as loud as he could behind him.

Logan came back over to the bed to sit beside me. He seemed pretty upset. I put my arm around him and grabbed his far shoulder with my hand, rubbing it soothingly. "Don't let what he says get to you. That's what he does when things don't go his way. He resorts to shouting and cursing like a fucking child," I explained to Logan, in an attempt to comfort him.

"I know...I'm surprised you've let it go on for this long. You said he's been this way for years?" He asked me.

I shrugged. "Yeah. He was like this before you came along. I guess I've gotten used to it over time. Look, everyone has their upsides and downsides. Garrett can be a grouch and go off the rail at times, but when he's in a good mood, he's a blast to be around. You've experienced that, right?"

Logan's face changed into a small, but brief, smirk. "Yeah. I guess so..."

I squeezed his shoulder, pressing his side into mine.

"And between you and me, I think that promise needed to go. It's been long overdue. I'm glad we did it. We broke the seal, so now we can do it more often." I confessed these thoughts to him.

Logan tilted his head to give me a peck on the lips. "I agree. I've been dying to have some one-on-one time with you."

The following morning, I was in the kitchen, making myself some iced coffee. Logan was still sound asleep upstairs. However, I heard footsteps coming downstairs. It was Garrett, dressed in a blue graphic t-shirt and gray running shorts. He held his tennis shoes in his hand and dropped them onto the floor by the kitchen door, leading to the garage.

He didn't utter a single word to me, nor did he bother to look at me. He simply went to the bathroom down the hall and came back into the kitchen.

"What are you up to?" I asked him.

"What's it look like?" He replied as he sat down and began putting on his shoes, tying them. Garrett didn't bother to glance in my direction.

"Are you going for a run or something?" I questioned him.

"Yeah. Duh!" He responded. "Trying something new. Gonna get myself back in shape. It's been long overdue."

Garrett normally didn't go for jogs or runs when he worked out. He was all about the weights. He performed very minimal cardio. And if he did anything cardio-related, it was usually on a bike. So, this caught me by surprise.

"Well, don't overexert yourself, Garrett. Don't forget about your heart. Routine exercise is good for people with AFib, but starting out heavy when your body isn't used to it..." Before I could finish explaining, I was immediately cut off by him.

"I got it. I got it. Sheesh!" He exclaimed.

I walked over to the refrigerator and opened it. I grabbed a bottle of water and tossed it to him. "Here. Catch. Make sure you stay hydrated. I'm serious!" I responded.

"Whatever you say, Doctor Pedrick." He opened the garage door and went out for the run.

Moments later, I heard another set of steps walking downstairs. This time, it was Logan, with his sexy bed-hair all over the place. He only had his underwear on. The sight of him increased my sexual appetite. He came over to kiss me.

"Good morning, babe," I said to him.

"Good morning. Was that Garrett that left? I heard the door shut," he replied.

"Yeah. He went for a quick run," I answered back to him.

"Oh…okay. Listen. I wanted to talk to you more, about last night." He briefly paused before continuing. "Do you think this whole thing is a mistake? That we've been moving too fast?" He asked.

"What? No. Of course not, Logan. I don't want you to ever think that." I wrapped my hands around him and held his smoldering, ass cheeks, before I continued on. "Look. Whether you were here or not, Garrett would be like this. That's just who he is. It has absolutely nothing to do with you. I was actually glad that you came into our lives when you did. And now, I can't picture my life without you, Logan," I confessed to him.

I could see the worry start to melt away from him as I gave him reassurance. We continued to talk more about last night, including the highs and lows of it. The conversation went on for a while before Logan interjected. "I'm gonna head upstairs and get showered for the day. Okay?" He let me know.

"Yeah. Sounds good." When he went upstairs, I decided to head into the office and work on my computer for a bit. I was right in the middle of typing up an email when my focus was interrupted by a knock at the front door. I proceeded to the foyer to answer it. When I opened the door, two police officers, one male and one female, stood before me. "Is this the residence of Garrett Pedrick?" The male officer asked.

I raised my brow at them, slightly befuddled with them being here. "Yes, it is. I'm Garrett's husband, Scott. What can I help you with? Is everything okay?" I asked with slight worry.

"Mr. Pedrick, Your husband is on his way to the hospital. One of your neighbors called 9-1-1 when they saw him pass out on the sidewalk, in front of their house. It looked to be some sort of stroke or heart attack," he stated.

I gasped in horror. This couldn't be real right now. Was this some sort of nightmare? Did I hear the cops, correctly? I stood in shock. "Are they heading to Freemont Memorial Hospital with him!?" I asked.

They both nodded. "Yes."

"My god…I need to…let me…I'll head over right now," I blurted to them. I could tell the officers felt extremely awkward and guilty at having to reveal this awful information to me.

"Sorry about giving you this news, Mr. Pedrick. This is the worst part of our jobs," the female officer announced. "We hate making these kind of house calls," she added.

I interrupted her. "No. I thank you for letting me know as soon as you could. But I really need to head over to the hospital now."

"No. We understand. I hope everything turns out okay. Have a good day, sir," the male cop stated.

This was their cue as they turned around and went back to their cars. I shut the door behind me and placed my back against it. I couldn't believe this was happening. I warned Garrett about overdoing it on the run.

Why the hell didn't he listen to me!?

I sprinted up the stairs and into the master bathroom, where I could hear the water running. Logan was rinsing himself off. I opened the glass shower door to make my presence known to him. "Hurry. We have to go, Logan. Garrett's in the hospital!"

"Oh my god! What!? What happened!?" Logan asked. He immediately turned the water off and came out, drying himself off.

I moved to our walk-in closet and started getting some clothes on, along with Logan. "The cops said a neighbor found him passed out on the sidewalk, from a stroke or heart attack," I explained.

"Holy fuck, Scott! I hope he's okay!" Logan stood up and moved over to hug me.

"Me too, Logan…me too."

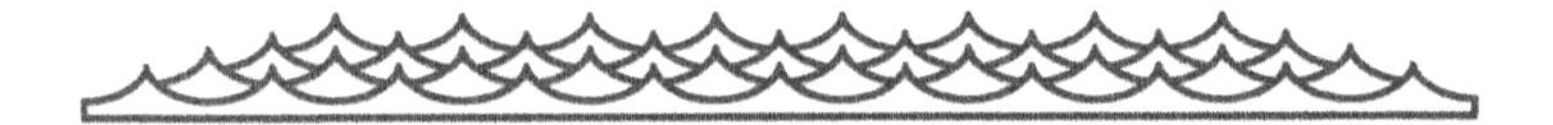

Logan and I arrived at Freemont Memorial Hospital. This was the same hospital where I completed my residency and where I first started off as a cardiologist, before launching my own practice. We sprinted to the receptionist, telling her we were here to see Garrett. She pointed us in the direction of the wing he was in. Logan and I made haste, hauling ass over there.

We found ourselves in the waiting room, patiently sitting, hoping a doctor would come out to greet us right away. Panic began to sink in, because of how long this was taking. I tried to bypass the nurses at the stand with my medical credentials, but they weren't accepting it. Even with me being a cardiologist, they wouldn't allow me back. "Hospital protocols," they referenced.

A doctor in a white coat soon emerged. "Dr. Pedrick?" he asked, searching around the room. As I stood up and he came closer to me, I recognized him. "Dr. Nassim!" I greeted him. We both worked together at Freemont in the past. It had been quite some time since I last communicated with him.

"You'll want to come with me," he declared. Logan stood up too and followed. Dr. Nassim addressed him. "And this is…?"

"A friend…here for support," I added. It would be too complicated to explain our whole relationship to Dr. Nassim. Plus, it was none of his business. So, I gave him the easiest answer I could, which he accepted. "Nice to meet you," he said to Logan. Then, he led us down the wing and into what looked like a small conference room with no one in it but the three of us now. The doctor shut the door behind him as we had a seat.

Fear began to strike. I realized Dr. Nassim was putting us in a private room to make sure we weren't around other visitors in the waiting room. This tended to mean that he didn't have good news to share. He came over and placed his hands on my shoulders.

"I'm sorry, Scott...Garrett didn't make it. There was nothing we could do. The stroke left him brain dead before he arrived at the hospital. And by then, it was too late..."

My heart sank into my stomach, once he revealed this.

My husband...was dead...

I placed my hands over my face and began to break down in tears. Logan rolled his chair over to me and held me in his arms, sobbing with me.

This couldn't be happening. This seriously couldn't be happening.

I kept repeating this to myself, hoping someone would pinch me or wake me up. But nothing. There was no change. This really was happening.

The doctor slowly started to back away to the door. "I'll leave you two alone for a moment. I'm so sorry, Scott." Dr. Nassim exited the room and shut the door behind him, leaving us in peace.

I continued to breathe heavily as I cried. I thought I was going to hyperventilate. I wrapped my arms around Logan, placing my head on his shoulder. My tears fell to his shirt as we held one another.

Garrett was gone...and there was nothing I could do about it.

Chapter 10

I sat at the funeral parlor, making final preparations with Garrett's family, for his burial. I had to take off work for a full two weeks to grieve. My lead technician, Cynthia, helped to reschedule all of my upcoming patient appointments. For those that had emergencies, I referred them to a nearby cardiologist. There was no way I could see patients, being in this state. I was not in the right frame of mind. I needed this time off.

There was a doom and gloom cloud, casted over our house for the past several days, since Garrett's death. Logan and I spent what seemed like endless nights, crying ourselves to sleep. At least we had each other to do it with. I couldn't bear the thought of going through this alone.

Garrett's family was extremely sympathetic towards me:

Garrett loved you so much, Scott.

You were amazing to him. You gave him a good life.

I'm so sorry, Scott. I can't imagine what you're going through right now.

Scott, please let us know if there's anything we can do for you.

These are rough times, Scott. You'll pull through. We'll all pull through.

These were some of the many condolences they offered me.

The day of the funeral had arrived. It was extremely tough to see my husband in a casket. He looked so beautiful though. Garrett rested in peace, in a light blue tuxedo. The hardest part about this experience was seeing all of our friends and family mourn with me.

They reminisced about old stories and memories they had of Garrett, which painted him in a nice light.

Logan sat in the back, preferring to be alone, during this entire experience. I understood how he was feeling. It would be too much for him to introduce himself to Garrett's family and friends as Garrett's other lover. He would have to explain that he had been Garrett's second boyfriend for nearly a year now and they knew nothing about it. It would be a very uncomfortable conversation to have, and to do it here of all places would be abysmal.

Pete and Lyle made their way over to me to pay their respects. Lyle moved to the back of the viewing room to sit with Logan and kept him company, leaving Pete and I alone to talk. He expressed his deepest condolences. "I'm sorry, Scott. Garrett was such a good guy. I can't even fathom how you must feel."

"Thanks, Pete. Yeah. It's been a rough couple of days. But thankfully, Logan and I have each other to share the burden with. We'll make it through this together," I added.

Pete gave me a blank stare. "About Logan, Scott. Is there a place we can go to, to talk for a moment? I don't want anyone to overhear us," he requested.

"Sure. I guess so. But let's make it quick. There are a lot of other people here I still haven't greeted and thanked yet," I mentioned.

Both of us walked out back and to the side of the funeral parlor, in the spare parking lot.

"Listen, Scott. I'm a little concerned for you, being with Logan," he confessed.

Where was he going with this?

I patted him on the shoulder. "Thanks, Pete. I appreciate it. But you don't need to be worried about us. We'll be fine," I clarified.

Pete shook his head. "No. That's not what I'm trying to say. Scott, don't you find it all a bit coincidental? Logan comes into your life and less than a year later, Garrett's found dead?" He asked.

I don't get it. This was so out of character for Pete. He knew of Garrett's history with his heart problems. Why was he making these accusations? Did he know something I didn't? Why was he so suspicious of Logan? There had to be a reason. But whatever that reason may be, I would never know. I was more annoyed that Logan was being attacked in this ruthless manner.

Pete was really crossing the line, and I was getting extremely pissed at his hint at Logan somehow being involved in this. It made me sick.

"Pete, you're really pushing the boundaries here, bud. Logan has been nothing but amazing since he got together with us. He has turned our lives upside down, for the better. Garrett's death was a horrible, freak accident. He had AFib. He was at high-risk of a stroke just from that alone. He hadn't exercised much and over-exerted himself. And I don't appreciate your accusations about Logan, who is completely innocent in all of this. He is just doing his best to try and mourn and deal with this as much as I am. Neither one of us need this kind of talk during my husband's funeral," I added with a bit of a flare in my voice.

Pete rubbed my shoulder. "I'm sorry, Scott. Forget I said any of this. I'm just trying to look out for you as your friend, is all. No bad intent, whatsoever. Please be smart though, and have your eyes peeled open when it comes to Logan. That's all I'm suggesting." He leaned in to give me a hug before stepping back. "I've taken up enough of your time. I'll let you get back to your guests," he said.

We both went back inside to the main gathering. I couldn't get what Pete had insinuated out of my head. I couldn't believe he assumed Logan had malintent. Logan didn't have a single malicious bone in his body. He has been nothing but kind, supportive, and generous to everyone in our lives. For Pete to have these thoughts about Logan was completely cruel. I assumed that Pete wasn't the only person with these ideas. That some of our other gay friends, who knew about us as a throuple, may have thought the same thing, and perhaps even had discussions about it behind our backs, especially if Pete had thought it too.

This was the last thing I wanted to hear from anyone. Logan didn't deserve it and neither did I. The more I thought about it, the angrier I got at Pete for bringing it up to me.

What a fucking asshole!

I made my way over to Logan to sit beside him on the red suede sofa to check in with him. "How are you holding up?" I inquired.

He let out a deep sigh. "I'm okay for now, I guess. A lot of our friends came up to me to show me support. That was really nice of them. How are you?" He asked.

"I'm okay. Listen…I had an idea. I've actually been thinking about it for the past two days. Once things settle down, why don't we take a vacation together? We need an escape from the house. A change of pace and a change of scene would do us both good. How does that sound?" I suggested.

He nodded. "That sounds like a nice idea. But let's talk about it later. I feel a bit guilty, having this conversation here, right now."

I simply nodded. "No. That makes sense. Anyway, I'm glad to hear everyone is treating you well and making you feel better. I'm gonna head back up front with the family. Come get me if you need anything." It took every cell in my body to control myself from giving him a kiss, right here, in front of everyone. I could see the expression across his face. He knew I wanted to do it but was aware that we wouldn't be able to in this public setting, with my and Garrett's families and friends among us.

I stood up and walked to the front. As I continued to talk with everyone that was around me, I found myself constantly looking over my shoulder at him. Not at Garrett like I should have been… but at Logan, instead.

Chapter 11

Two weeks after Garrett's funeral, Logan and I decided to take that vacation together like I had suggested. Although I was only supposed to be out of the office for two weeks, I extended the time off for an additional week, so Logan and I could venture out of the country together. It was much needed.

We were both in a slump around the house for the past several weeks as I imagined. We did go out to dinner a few times, but our thoughts and conversations immediately shifted back to Garrett, every time we attempted to bring up a different subject. Logan and I only had sex once in the past two weeks. I mean, that's what I should have expected, right? Most people don't have sex within two weeks of their spouse dying. But as much as my brain was telling me this, my heart and my cock were narrating a different story. I still found myself longing and yearning for Logan's body. I needed to feel his warm, silky skin on me and desperately longed to be inside him. So, this vacation couldn't have come at a better time.

As for where we were traveling to, I left that up to Logan. I let him have the reins, allowing him to research some places and book our flights, hotel, and expenses, at a capped price of course.

Right now, we dipped our feet into the warm, white sands of Playa Delfines beach in Cancún, Mexico. I gazed out into the distance of what seemed like endless crystal, blue water. Logan was sporting a tight, ruby red, speedo with matching red sunglasses. I wore a gray and white striped speedo to complement him.

We sat back in our beach chairs, taking in the beautiful weather that we were experiencing. The palm-leaf umbrella that hovered over us, provided a nice shade. It was our second day here in Cancún. If our first night was any indication of how this vacation would continue to go, I was beyond eager to see what the rest of the trip had in store for us.

Logan and I had sex for nearly three hours straight last night, in our hotel suite. We couldn't seem to keep our hands off of each other. Our bodies wrapped up together in a permanent, warm, and passionate embrace was an experience we never wanted to end. But sadly, all good things must come to an end. I hated separating myself from him, but I really didn't have a choice in the matter.

Logan had a few tricks up his sleeve for this vacation. He said there were many surprises he had planned for us, during our stay here. But I would just have to wait until they were sprung on me. He promised I would love each and every one of them. We'll see how they turn out. I had nothing but the greatest confidence in him and his excursion choices.

I drifted my attention down to my hand, which Logan now held tightly.

"So, I have a confession to make," I announced.

Logan took his sunglasses off and put them on his head, staring at me. I could see I had his full and undivided attention as I said this.

"What sort of confession?" He asked.

"Nothing bad, of course. But I do need to take control of this trip, just this once," I explained.

Logan had a perplexed expression on his face. "What do you mean?"

"Well, I have dinner planned for us, tonight. But I promise, this is the only surprise I planned for us. You can have every other dinner planned out," I clarified.

Logan cracked up. "You can't help yourself, can you? But, yes. That's fine, babe," he added as he leaned over across the arm of his beach chair to kiss me.

I returned the favor. "Okay. But we should start wrapping it up out here. We need showers and I expect you in dress clothes," I commanded.

"Oh? We're going fancy tonight?" He asked.

"Something like that," I replied.

After we returned to our hotel room and cleaned ourselves up, I made my way down to the hotel bar alone. Logan still needed some time to finish getting ready for our dinner date. I was dressed to the nines this evening. I had on a black suit and tie with a white shirt. My hair was slick and gelled back. I had the James Bond look going on tonight and I was pretty pleased as I checked myself out in the lobby mirror, on my way to the bar.

I sat at the counter as the bartender approached me. "What can I get you?" He asked.

"A bourbon on the rocks," I requested.

"Any preference in bourbon?" He inquired.

"Yeah." I popped my head to the side to get a good look at the bourbon selection that was behind the counter. "I'll take the Woodford Reserve."

"Coming right up," the bartender responded.

I stared up at him and saw his eyes widen as he glared behind me. He practically looked starstruck. I spun around in my stool to see what had caught his attention. Was it a celebrity? No. It was a guy in tight, gray dress pants. His figure was enticing. He wore a fitted, white button-down shirt with it. His wrist-cuffs were folded back, revealing a shiny, silver Armani watch he was sporting. His hair was spiked up, immaculately.

My face beamed as I recognized the man. He was my man!

Logan sat beside me in the empty stool at the bar. He sat forward as the bartender spoke to him. I subtly leaned back to get the perfect view of that sexy ass of his, which looked fucking phenomenal in those tight, gray dress pants he was wearing.

"What will it be?" The bartender asked him.

"Let's go with an extra dirty martini for now. Make it vodka," Logan added.

"Any choice in the vodka?"

"Do you have Grey Goose?" Logan inquired.

"Definitely!" The bartender replied.

"Perfect. I'll take that," he responded.

As the bartender finished making our drinks and handed them off to us, Logan held his drink out to me. "Let's make a toas…" He paused. His face did a complete one-eighty and I sensed a sadness in him.

What happened?...Oh shit!

I realized that giving a toast was Garrett's thing. Logan was instantly reminded of him the second he suggested giving one. I attempted to cheer him up with some encouragement, by holding my glass up to his. "I think he would want you to make a toast, Logan. I think he would enjoy that, a lot."

Logan smiled at me. "I think so too. So, here's to an amazing trip together and of course to Garrett. He will forever be in our hearts," he added, with a tear in his eye.

I clinked my glass with his. "Cheers!" I exclaimed. We both sipped on our drinks.

"So, why don't we bring our drinks with us?" I recommended.

"Bring them with us? To where?" He asked.

"Not far. Just follow me," I suggested.

We left the bar area and went outside, beyond the hotel. We walked down the pier toward the beach. As we approached, there were candles surrounding a table for two, with a white, circular table cloth draped over it and white chairs. Rose petals were scattered across the top of it with other taller candles displayed. A bottle of champagne sat in an ice bucket on top of the table. It was beyond romantic.

Logan placed his hands over his mouth in surprise. "Scott!? You planned this? How? We were out here like two hours ago?"

I shrugged. "It's magic, I guess."

I held his hand as we walked across the sand and arrived at the lit table. I pulled out his chair for him to sit, while I moved to sit in the other one. As we sat down, I popped the champagne bottle and quickly poured it into our crystal flutes, before it could overflow onto the table.

We took sips before placing them back down.

"You didn't have to do all of this, Scott," he said as if he was the one imposing.

"What? You don't like it?" I asked.

"No. I absolutely love it! Every bit of it!" He clarified.

"Good!" I replied.

We were interrupted as three waiters came over with appetizers and expensive steaks. They plated both of us and headed back up to the pier towards the hotel.

"Mmmmm. This is incredible!" Logan exclaimed, taking his first bite of the steak.

I didn't even let him finish his bite, before I put him on the spot. I got up from my seat and then knelt down in front of him, with one knee in the sand. "Logan, I know I've said it so many times already, but I seriously can't say it enough. I am beyond blessed to have you in my life, and I can't picture not having you in it. You have bewitched me, body and soul, since the day we met. I know the timing of this is a bit odd, but it feels so right, and I would be lying to myself if I withheld these feelings any longer." I paused my speech and reached into my pocket to pull out a small black box. I opened it, revealing an engagement band. The candlelight reflected off the one carat diamonds that were embedded in the ring. It was 10K white gold.

Logan placed his hands over his mouth, completely shocked at my gesture.

"Logan Rippling…will you be my husband and make me the happiest man alive?"

I could see the tears start to swell up in his eyes when he nodded. "Yes! A hundred times yes, Scott!" He held out his hand to me so I could place the ring on his finger. He held his hand up and towards the lit candles, at the center of the table, to get a better look at the ring. He got out of his seat and knelt down in the sand with me, grabbing my face with his hands to passionately kiss me. Losing our balance, we wound up falling into the sand. Both of us were holding each other and rolling around, kissing one another, playing the fall off as if we had planned it.

"I think Logan Pedrick has a nice ring to it. Don't you think?" I asked.

"It does. It really does!" He responded. "But doesn't Scott Rippling sound better?"

I laughed. "It sure does."

Later that night, Logan and I made love to each other when we got back to the hotel room. We could barely finish dinner. We were desperate and itching to get some privacy so that we could fuck. It was another long session of kissing, touching, groping, sucking, and fucking. I held him in my arms afterwards and we slowly drifted off to sleep.

I had thoughts about Garrett that night, and knew that deep down, he would want this for Logan and me. It was the right thing to do. Garrett's memory would live with me forever.

I would now have a new husband. Another marriage was on the horizon. As for this new husband, well…I was able to turn him from a pool boy into a man.

Part II
Logan

Chapter 12

"Logan, we're gonna do a round of lemon drop shots. You in!?" My friend Skyler Steller asked me this, while he and our friend Zach came over to me at the bar, returning from the dance floor. Zach and Skyler were home from college for the summer. While they were home, we often went out to gay clubs together. Well, *gay club friends* was the more appropriate title, because that's the only time I ever saw them, was if we were out at a bar or club.

"Are you seriously fucking asking me that!? Of course I do!" I shouted to get my voice above the loud sound of the club remix playing, so they could both hear me. The sexy bartender winked at me, handing us the shots, and down the hatch they went.

This was already my sixth shot of the night and my fourth mixed drink. It wasn't even past eleven yet. Skyler was soon dragged into a conversation with some douchebag looking guy, leaving Zach Cauderling and I alone. Zach wrapped his arm around me. "So, what are you up to, later on tonight?" He asked me.

I shrugged. "Not sure. Either getting laid or going home…or maybe a combination of both if I'm the only one that can host." I laughed at my own comment and Zach joined in.

"Well, if you want to make sure that happens, I'm sure we can work something out." He reached his hand under my shirt to rub my abs, hinting this to me.

I rolled my eyes at him and pushed his hand off me. "No thanks, Cauderling! The last time we fucked, you got weird as hell at the end when I tried to cum. You didn't want to be touched. I don't play that kind of game," I replied to him.

"Oh, come on, Logan. That was a one-time thing. I swear," he pleaded.

"Nah. Maybe another time. You are sexy as fuck though." I leaned in to bite his bottom lip, before I continued, "I'll give you that."

Zach had a devious grin on his face after I bit him. "Fucking little cock tease! Suit yourself. There may not be *another time* if you turn me down. I may not be so willing in the future," he threatened.

Zachary Cauderling loved to play mind games with people. I easily gathered that from the very first time we met. It was too bad he didn't know who he was fucking with. And I was more than capable of fucking him over than he realized.

"I think I'll take my chances." I ended the discussion with that and headed off to the bathroom. I locked myself in the last stall and faced the toilet, spreading my legs, pretending to take a piss. Instead, I pulled out a key and a small dime bag of cocaine. Opening it, I poured the white substance onto the key and held it up to my nose, to snort it. I closed my eyes and slightly tilted my head back to let the rush hit me.

I tossed the small baggie into the toilet, before I kicked the handle to flush it. Down the drain the evidence went. I came back out of the stall and headed back to the bar area. I was the only one there now. Skyler and Zach must have run off and disappeared somewhere else in the club. I sat at the bar and looked around. I desperately wanted another drink, but I didn't want to have to pay for it.

No fucking way!

As hot and sexy as I was, there should be no need for me to ever have to buy my own drink. I refused to. I glanced over my shoulder to see a few guys staring at me. Now it was a matter of selecting one of these stupid schmucks that would be dumb enough to actually think I was interested in getting to know them.

I continued to make eye contact with the middle-aged guy in the red Abercrombie shirt that looked like it was one size too small for him. As soon as I did this, he made his way over to the bar and sat in the stool next to me.

It was like taking candy from a fucking baby.

In this case, it was a balding, middle-aged man, still trying to pull off an Abercrombie polo, thinking he still was a fucking baby. "Hey gorgeous," he said to me.

"Hi," was the only word I gave him.

"I've seen you around here a few times. You're hard to forget," he confessed.

I put my hand on his knee. "Awww. That's really nice of you to say." The pitch in my voice was a little higher than usual, as I said this to him.

"I'm Dylan. And you are…?" He paused to let me finish his sentence.

"Kenny. Nice to meet you, Dylan," I replied.

I never liked giving my real name out to random guys. I had my fair share of crazy, psycho stalkers in the past. They'd find me on Instagram and message me every five seconds. Sometimes, they'd DM me up to fifty times, without me once responding to them. It was then that I realized they couldn't take the hint and I was forced to block them. I didn't even want to look at my *blocked list.* God only knows how long that list was.

Dylan stood up and leaned over the counter until he got the bartender's attention.

"You need a drink?" The bartender asked him.

"Yeah. Can I get a Bud Light and whatever he wants?" He pointed his thumb to me as he stated this, before I spoke up.

"I'll have a rum and coke," I added.

The bartender made our drinks and returned to us, handing me my mixed drink and giving Dylan his bottle of Bud Light.

Ewww. Fucking Bud Light. Who goes to a gay bar and orders a Bud Light? A fucking schmuck, that's who.

I continued to judge this loser, while he attempted to get to know me.

"So? You live around here? Go to school?" His questions felt like more of an interrogation, and I was getting terribly bored with it.

I pulled out my phone and pretended to read a text message in front of him. "Oh! My friend Jake just messaged me. I told him I'd meet up with him. He's on the bar side of the club," I lied.

"Ahhh. Okay. Well, I'll let you go. Do you want to exchange phone numbers or…?" Dylan asked.

Ugh! Leave me the fuck alone and let me go already! Christ!

"Ummm. I usually don't give out my number after first meeting someone. But maybe the next time I run into you here, we can make the exchange?" I suggested.

"Alright. Well then, see ya around gorgeous."

I got out of my seat and walked slightly off-balanced to the other end of the club, to the bar side. I circled the bar to see that no one worthwhile was around. It was just the same old queens that came here practically every weekend. There were no hot guys nor men that looked like they were rich, who piqued my interest. It was simply a dull dud-fest tonight.

I was bored and decided that I was going to end the night early. I called for an Uber and left the club. I got in the backseat of the car, after the driver pulled up in his black SUV. We drove off. As I sat, I responded to a few missed text messages and browsed around on social media feeds. I glanced up from my phone and saw that the driver was watching me through his rear-view mirror.

He immediately turned his attention back to the road, realizing I had caught him staring at me. From what I could see of him from behind, he was pretty decent looking. I'd say a little above average.

Looked to be in his mid-thirties. I was able to catch the gold wedding band on his left hand when he placed it on top of the steering wheel.

"So, you come out here often?" The driver asked me, trying to have some small talk.

I can't believe it took him a whole five minutes to start a conversation, but my guess was that was because he didn't want it to seem awkward, after I saw him glancing at me.

"Yeah. Only when I'm meeting friends out here for dinner or to hit up one of the bars and clubs in the area," I answered back.

"Ahhh. Gotcha. Well, that's cool. My wife and I recently moved into the area with our six-month-old."

"Nice..." was all I replied to him with.

I diverted my attention back down to my phone, while he continued to drive. We were only about ten minutes away from my apartment building. I stared up for a second and, once again, I caught him checking me out in the mirror. His gaze moved away the second he saw me catch him.

I can't say I was surprised he was doing this. Men were always captivated by me. It didn't matter whether they were gay or straight, but I received all sorts of stares from everyone. I'm not sure if it was because of my face, my body, or what. But I've had my fair share of closeted, married men with wives, who hit on me. I assumed this was the case now.

I'll admit, I was a little buzzed from the crazy amount of drinks I had at the bar. Plus, I can't recall that I've ever actually had sex with an Uber driver before. There was just something about me being able to sway people's minds and manipulate them that absolutely fucking thrilled me. It was like a game to me. The more extreme the situation was, where I would manage to get my way, the more exciting it was. Getting drinks paid for by men and getting hot sex from closeted straight men were merely small feats. But getting expensive jewelry bought for me and bills paid for by men were harder challenges that I somehow managed to accomplish. I knew how to use my body and charm to get ahead in life. It was all second nature to me.

I started to have some dirty thoughts about the idea of this driver pulling over to a private spot somewhere, in the middle of the night, and having his way with me. The concept really turned me on. I could feel my cock start to rise as I continued to let my imagination run wild with this idea.

I decided to try and push my luck with him. "Yeah. That's nice you have a wife and kid. I'm single," I found myself saying aloud to him.

"Oh…really? I mean, you're a pretty good-looking dude. That's kind of surprising," he responded.

Now I was getting somewhere with him. I just needed to push a little more and let him know how fuckable I was. That was the thing with these types of encounters with straight men. They totally wanted the sex and wanted to fuck me on the DL, but they feared rejection and also the potential risk of being exposed. So, I had to make it known to him, at least with a few hints, that I was interested in getting fucked by him and that I would keep it a secret.

"Thanks. Well, I really put it on myself. I'm not a committed sort of guy. You know what I mean?" I asked.

"Yeah. I guess that makes sense." He glanced up at me through the rear-view mirror once again. This time, however, when he saw me, I was slouched down in the seat with my legs a little more spread apart.

I nodded to him. "Uh huh. I just like to have sex a lot. Can't help it."

He was becoming more interested in our conversation. "To each their own. So, how often do you have sex?" He asked.

"About three times a week, maybe?" I exaggerated a little bit with this answer. It was usually only once every week or two I had sex with someone, but again, I was playing this brave game with him. I needed to continue to make myself seem fuckable to him, to see if he would actually take the bait.

"Damn! That's a lot! I barely fuck my wife but once a month now," he confessed.

Now it was time to reel this fish in.

"Ouch. Yeah...that sucks. There's no way I could go past one week without getting fucked," I mentioned.

"Gotcha. So, how do you get so many guys? Are they regular fuck buddies of yours, or strangers?"

"Strangers most of the time. I usually meet them online, on Grindr," I answered.

"Yeah. I've heard of it before," he admitted.

"Mhmm. It's been a good week since I last had sex. So, I'm definitely looking to get fucked tonight," I bravely added.

This was the final trigger I pulled. I was anxious to see how he would respond to it. He locked eyes with me again, through the mirror, as I told him this.

"Have you ever been fucked by a married guy before?" He asked.

Boom! I deserved a fucking Academy Award!

This made me know he was really considering fucking me. So, I let him know he would be safe if he did. "Yeah. Quite a few, actually. But their secret is always safe with me. I never kiss and tell," I assured him.

The driver remained silent for a moment. I could tell he was contemplating his decision. I rubbed my cock through the outside of my pants, hoping he would catch me in the act.

"Do you have your place to yourself, or do you know of a private spot we could go to?" He asked.

Holy fuck! This was seriously happening right now!

"Yeah. If you make a right down this road and your next left onto Groudermill Road, there's a park on the right-hand side we can pull into."

He did as I instructed and drove through the parking lot towards the very back of the park. There were no cars or people in sight, which was to be expected. It was past midnight, after all. The only lights we saw were shining on the bare baseball fields that were off in the distance.

"So, how do you want to do this?" He asked while unbuckling his belt.

"I don't care. Why don't you hop in the back here with me and we can start there?" I suggested.

He got out of the SUV and had me do the same. The driver pulled the seats down so that the entire back of the vehicle was a large flat surface that extended to the trunk.

We both jumped into the back. He shut the door behind him.

I laid on my back as he crawled on top of me and started kissing me on the lips. His hand reached under my shirt to get a good feel of my body.

"You are one sexy little slut!" He whispered into my ear.

"Thanks. You're not so bad yourself," I returned the compliment.

His hands pulled my shirt over my head and I helped him take his off as well. We rushed to take our shoes off, unbuckle our belts and stripped down, completely naked. Time was of the essence with him still being on his Uber shift. Also, we faced the risk of someone passing by on a nightly stroll, who could catch us in the act.

Now that we were both exposed to each other, he moved on top of me once again, and leaned down to taste my lips. I opened my mouth for him, allowing his tongue to enter it, to meet mine. I could feel his nice, hairy chest rub against my smooth skin. This whole scene was beyond fucking hot. I was so aroused right now.

We continued to kiss for a while, before I wiggled my way out from under him. "I wanna taste that thick dick of yours," I told him.

He turned over on his back and I knelt in front of him. I began jerking him off with my hand, but I didn't have to for very long to get him erect. He was already as hard as a rock. I spit on his cock and placed my mouth over it, sucking him off like a ravaged maniac.

"Fuck!!! That's amazing, boy!" He yelled. I felt him grab my legs and twist my body around, so that my ass was on top of his face as I continued to blow him.

"Mmmmm! Shit!" I gasped and stopped sucking him off for a moment, feeling his slippery tongue on my asshole. I turned my head to look over my shoulder, to watch him eat me out. It felt so fucking good! I went back to servicing his dick with my mouth. We were 69ing each other and it was satisfying as hell.

"You have the sexiest fucking ass I've ever seen!" He confessed.

After a few minutes, he pulled his face out from my ass. "You ready to get fucked, boy?" He asked me.

I unwrapped my lips from his dick to reply to him. "Yes, daddy. I want your big fucking cock in me! I want it bad!" As I stated this, I rolled off him.

It was a pretty tight space in the back of his SUV. He got up and kneeled, which gave me more room to now get down on all fours and bend my ass out in the air for him. He moved closer to it, ready to fuck me.

"Jesus! That ass is out of this world!" He smacked it hard and squeezed my cheeks with his hands. "Here it comes, boy!" His raw dick pressed into me. I could feel him buried inside me.

"Fuck!" I yelled. We didn't have any lube on us, so I would have to tolerate the pain for a bit and get used to it. For the first minute, it ached, but when he picked up his rhythm with fucking me, it felt so much better. My hand reached for my own cock to jack it off as he relentlessly continued to pound my hole.

"Damn, that ass is tight! You like daddy's dick in you, boy!?"

"Yes. I fucking love that dick in me, daddy!" I shouted.

"You want daddy's cum in you?" He asked.

"Yes daddy, I want that fucking cum in me. I want you to breed me, daddy!" I told him.

"Fuck. Here it comes boy! Argghhhh!" He grunted hard as I felt his jizz shoot deep inside me.

The sound of his dominance put me over the edge. I stroked my dick faster until I completely splooged all over his back seat.

He pulled out of me slowly. As soon as he did, my legs gave out and I collapsed onto my stomach. My chest was rising and falling deeply, as I breathed.

"That was fucking hot!" He smacked my ass hard, before grabbing it with his hand to jiggle it.

"I'd fuck that ass everyday if I could," he admitted.

I simply turned around and smiled at him. I started grabbing my underwear and clothes to put back on. My cumshot was all across the back of his seat. He could tell I was staring at it. "Don't worry about it. I'll clean it up later," he explained.

The driver proceeded to put his own clothes back on. He opened the door and we both hopped out of the car, so that he could return the backseats to their normal positions. I motioned to get in the back to sit there, but he held is arm up to prevent me from doing so.

"You can sit in the front seat, you know?" He suggested.

Fuck! I just wanted to sit in the backseat and get home. Why did this now have to turn into one of those awkward post-fuck sessions?

"Sure," I simply said, before I opened the passenger side door and climbed in, as this guy recommended.

He got in on the driver's side and turned on the GPS on his phone, driving back to my apartment. During the drive, he kept his right hand on my inner thigh and kept squeezing it, during the entire car ride home.

I didn't bother to remove his hand from me. I was in no position to do that, as much as I had wanted to. After all, he was my ride home. I didn't want to be forced to walk home, even if it was a twenty minute or so walk from where we were currently at.

He turned his black SUV into my apartment complex. As he stopped the car in the middle of the parking lot, he stretched his seatbelt and leaned over to kiss me on the lips. I instantly pulled away the second he did it.

What the fuck was that!?

I opened the car door and brushed off his attempted kiss. I was still nice to him. "Thanks for the ride...*both* rides, I mean." I winked at him and jumped out of the car.

"No problem. I'll see you around, I guess," he replied.

"Yeah. See you around." I shut the car door and walked towards the entrance of my apartment building.

I definitely wouldn't be seeing him around. That was for fucking sure.

I reflected on how the night went as I entered the lobby and headed up the elevator, to my floor. What started off as a fairly boring night at the club turned into a hot, fantasy car sex scene. I was now satisfied with how the night panned out.

After getting fucked that hard, I was ready for my beauty sleep, not that I needed to gain any *extra* beauty or anything. I already had that.

Chapter 13

After the wild Uber sex, I found myself in my studio apartment, sitting up in my bed. I was in my underwear, ready to go to sleep, but ultimately decided to get on my cell phone and search through a few Instagram feeds, before hitting the sack.

Most of the posts of the gay men I followed were all the same. I scrolled through countless images of thots in their speedos by the pool or on the beach, desperate for attention. *Bleh*! Pictures of boys pretending to cook nice meals. *Gag*! Scenes of guys in front of old stone architectural buildings of some sort. *Demolish it!*

My profile picture was of me in a dark blue speedo, but I was way hotter and attractive than those dirty, little twink thots on the beach.

I returned back to my home-page and saw a new notification. It was a message from a random, hot man that started following me, earlier. His name was *Garrett Pedrick*. I decided to entertain him.

I went to Garrett's profile to search through his pictures. He was sexier than I had imagined. A bit older than me, but nevertheless. He looked pretty rich from what I gathered. There were pictures of him on tons of vacations and at fancy dinners with whom I assumed was his boyfriend or husband. I read through the captions in order to confirm that it was, indeed, his husband. The sexy husband wasn't tagged in any of the photos though, making me realize he probably must not have had an Instagram. But seeing how extravagant this man's lifestyle was, really had me intrigued. I continued to message him back.

Our chat continued with more sexual compliments and things we were going to do to each other in bed tomorrow, when we met. I also provided Garrett with my address. Once our conversation died down, I found myself constantly navigating back to his pictures. He lived this exuberant, affluent lifestyle that I was drawn to. I was able to get more information from his Instagram posts. His husband must have been some sort of doctor. There were images from years ago, of them at medical conferences, him with his arms around his husband, who was in a white doctor's coat, and another picture of him and his husband in front of a clinic or medical building of some sort with the caption:

So proud of Scott for officially opening up his own practice. #gaysuccess

I reflected on the comment Garrett made about him and his husband's situation. That they were supposedly in an *open relationship* and messed around with other people and didn't talk about it with each other. This was complete and utter bullshit. The oldest trick in the book. Just who the hell did he take me for?

The writing on the wall was crystal clear. He cheated on his husband frequently and kept it a secret. He used the excuse of being in an open relationship to make it easier for himself to come onto other men and sleep with them. But what can I say? This didn't stop me. I was still interested in him. I stalked his account a little while longer.

Now, getting the opportunity to meet and mess around with Garrett was something I was becoming more and more obsessed with. I wanted to not only have sex with him, but I wanted to be his friend and get closer to him, period. I wished I had his life, and I was determined to have his lifestyle. How could he be married and that wealthy and happy, yet be chatting it up with other men online and cheat on his husband? He didn't deserve all that he had. If anyone deserved it, it was *me*!

Yet here this cheating scumbag was, living the life. If it was attainable for him, then it could be attainable for anyone, right? I continued scrolling through what seemed like countless photos of Garrett, some with his husband, and some with their friends. I literally searched every single one of Garrett's friends that he tagged in his photos, including another doctor named Pete and his partner Lyle.

Maybe I was envious of Garrett with his large group of friends, wealth, and glamorous vacations he took. I couldn't keep my eyes off of his profile. I pictured myself in his shoes. I wanted all of that for *me*.

I felt like a mad man, now captivated with this *life* I wasn't a part of. And I was now determined to be a part of *that life*.

Chapter 14

It was an hour before Garrett was expected to arrive at my apartment for the very first time. I hopped in the shower and freshened up. I made sure to shave every crevice of my body. I was already pretty smooth to begin with, but I wanted to make sure my skin was extra smooth and silky for this alluring man.

After getting out of the shower and drying off, I went to my underwear drawer. I was in a dilemma, unsure of what to wear. Should I go with a jock-strap, some tight Andrew Christian underwear, or the Calvin Kleins? No. None of them. I picked up one of my pairs of Danny Miami underwear, holding it up. It had a gold waistband, while the bulk of the underwear was white, with some gold patterns on it. I put them on and stared at myself in the mirror posing from the front and the back. I bent over, pleased with how well they made my ass stand out.

Surprisingly, that was actually the easier decision to make. Now, it was time to pick what shirt and pants to wear. I skimmed through the clothes hanging in my closet, uncertain of how to dress for the occasion. Should I get all dressed up, or maybe go with sweatpants for easy access? No. That was out of the question. Garrett Pedrick was a wealthy man. So, I needed to dress to impress him. This led me to pull out a pair of dark blue, slim-fit dress pants and a white button-down shirt. Now, I had to come up with an excuse as to why I was wearing this outfit around the apartment, when he arrived. I would have to give it some thought.

I already spent all morning tidying up the place, although there wasn't exactly much to straighten out. My studio apartment was only

600 square feet. I wasn't ashamed of it by any means. It had a very nice view of the city and I decorated it nicely. Plus, this was only a temporary residence, while I was in college.

I was studying Human Services, which was a broad field. I honestly had no fucking clue what I wanted to do once I graduated with my degree. I do love wine, so maybe I could get into the sommelier business? I definitely had the sexy, debonair look down pat for it. That was a given. Maybe I could go into hospitality? Not sure. However, if nothing worked out, I could easily fall back into being a model or a porn star. I was approached by multiple people and agents over the past several years, begging to sign me, but I turned them all down.

No. I had bigger hopes and dreams. Bigger fish to fry. I needed to find a rich man. A sugar daddy who would spoil the living hell out of me. Ultimately, that's what I wanted. I could see that Garrett had that, and I wanted it too, badly!

I had about another half an hour to kill before he got here. I checked my cell phone and found myself going back to Instagram and to Garrett's profile. I went through more of his images again. It was maddening. I was becoming obsessed with this guy and I hadn't even met him yet. What was wrong with me?

A message soon popped up on my screen.

On my way. Be there in five min.

The butterflies fluttered in my stomach as I read this. I was now getting a little giddy and antsy, knowing I would be meeting him in person for the first time, at any moment. Finally, there was a knock at the door a few minutes later. I opened it and there he was, in the living flesh, Garrett Pedrick. His pictures did not do him justice. His brown hair was spiked in a really sexy way. His body was tan and toned. However, he wasn't as dressed up as me, which I found quite surprising. He simply wore a pair of blue jeans and a green graphic t-shirt.

He greeted me the second I opened the door. "Hey! Logan, right?"

I nodded. "The one and only! Haha. Come on in."

Garrett walked into the center of the room and I closed the front door behind him. I could see he was spinning around, getting a good look at my place, already making judgments.

This left me a little embarrassed, so I felt the need to explain my situation. "Yeah. This is just a rental while I'm in college."

"No…it's really charming," Garrett admitted.

This made me feel less insecure. I sat down on my couch and rubbed the spot next to me, wanting him to do the same. "Here. Have a seat," I instructed.

He plopped himself down right beside me. I noticed he was admiring my outfit or my body. Hell, probably both. "You're dressed really nicely," he observed.

"Thanks. I had a presentation at college I gave this morning. No big deal," I lied. But it made me sound responsible, smart, and prestigious, all at the same time. It was just one of the many lies I had up my sleeve that was on the menu.

"So, what do you do for work?" I asked him.

"I work for an insurance company. I'm an agent," he replied.

This confirmed my suspicions that Garrett's husband, Scott, was the clear breadwinner in their relationship. There was absolutely no fucking way Garrett could afford his lavish lifestyle off of an insurance agent's salary. Far from it. Scott was his sugar daddy, and I was completely jealous of it. Jealous that he managed to find a hot, rich, and successful man, which was my goal in the long run. But I deserved it more than he did. Here he was, cheating on his husband. I would be faithful, as fucking ever.

"That's cool," I replied.

Garrett then placed his hand on my leg, rather abruptly. "Let's cut the small talk," he recommended.

"Sounds good to me. I'm ready whenever you are," I let him know.

He instantly leaned in to kiss me. I closed my eyes and welcomed his lips with my own. He moved on top of me, pushing me back into the sofa. I wrapped my legs around him when he did this, rubbing my socks down the back of his calves.

"You are without a doubt, the sexiest fucking thing I've ever seen," he complimented me.

"You're so fucking hot too," I returned.

Garrett sat back to take his shoes and socks off, followed by his shirt and jeans, allowing me to see the black underwear he had on. I followed in suit, unbuttoning my dress shirt, before pulling off my pants and socks. I moved to the bed across the room and laid down on it. He followed me. I was expecting him to join me, but I saw that he had stopped to stand at the foot of the bed, gazing at me. Garrett's body was undeniably attractive. However, now that I knew Scott was the one with the money in their relationship and that Garrett hung onto his coattails, my attraction to him was diminished. But I knew going along with this would get me going in the right direction in getting to hang out with them. So, there was no going back.

"Jesus Christ! You're unbelievable, Logan," he said, continuing to stare at me, captivated by my body. I simply gave him a smirk, before he kneeled on the bed and sprawled out on top of me. He was in the perfect position to kiss me passionately.

I traced my hands across his chest and lower torso, touching the curves of his muscles. His kisses left my lips and started to head south on my neck, and down my chest, towards my stomach. When he did this, I could feel his fingers against my hips, grabbing the waistband of my underwear to pull them off.

"Nice!" He exclaimed, now seeing my dick for the first time.

Garrett immediately put his mouth on it and began blowing me. The warmth of his breath on my cock felt so fucking good. I took in a deep breath and moaned. "Mmmm."

He moved his tongue down to my balls, licking and sucking on them, while he clenched his hand into a fist to grasp and jerk my dick off.

Garrett continued to work my cock. I stretched my arm to grab the bottle of lube on the wooden side table and placed it next to us in bed, knowing we would be needing it, any second from now.

Actually, it would be less time than that. Garrett instantaneously seized the bottle and drenched his fingers with it. He returned to blowing me, but this time, he massaged the crease of my smooth ass. It was so sensual and intense. That feeling was heightened once I felt him press inside to finger me. He wiggled and dug deeper, teasing my prostate, while his tongue simultaneously stimulated my dick. My hands tugged on my bedsheets and I began arching my back, wanting him to get his finger deeper in me, although I'm not sure that was even possible with how far he was in already. I was on the verge of cumming.

"Slow down…I'm gonna cum," I pleaded.

A devilish grin displayed across his face. Instead of decreasing the pace, he went full throttle and rapidly shook his finger inside me.

What the fuck!? Oh my god! I can't take it anymore!!!

I shot so hard. The cum gushed across my chest and hit me in the face. I panted to catch my breath and closed my eyes, in an attempt to relax my body and muscles.

But little did I know, they were being put to work once again. I yelled loudly in pleasure, as I felt something plug into my ass. This time, it was Garrett's thick, raw cock. He smiled at me and began thrusting. "We're not done yet. I'm gonna make you cum again," he whispered with a slight growl.

What!? There was no way I would be able to do that!

As much as I wanted to rest and relax my body, it began to have a mind of its own and take control over me. I was fully submitting to Garrett's dominant behavior.

Garrett continued to fuck me, while stroking my dick with his hand. "Damn! This is the tightest, fucking ass I've ever been in. I don't know how long I'm gonna last," he confessed.

"Then cum in me, baby. I want your hot load inside me," I admitted.

"No. I'm not gonna cum until you do, again," he explained.

Fuck! He was relentless!

But much to my surprise, I felt my dick hardening once again. His cock felt amazing in me. My ass muscles clenched around it, holding onto it for dear life as he motioned in and out of me. I wanted Garrett so badly in this moment. I wanted his cock, his body, and now I wanted him to breed me. The thought of it made me wild and I couldn't believe what was happening. A surge was running down my spine.

"Shit! I'm gonna cum again! What the fuckkkk!!!???" And I shot my second load, not even five minutes after my first cumshot. The sight of it must have made Garrett hit his limit, because I could feel his dick pulsate inside me.

He let out a deep, prolonged grunt as he released himself in my hole. Garrett fell on top of me, but still kept his dick in my ass. He clasped my cheek with his hands and started making out with me again. "You are fucking insatiable, Logan. My god…" he said, seductively.

"Mmmm. That was unbelievable. I could let you fuck me every day," I let him know.

"Well, why don't we?" He suggested.

"Huh? You mean fuck every day?" I asked, somewhat confused.

"Well, not every day, but we can make it a regular thing," he explained.

"Yeah. That sounds good to me. I can't get enough of that dick," I replied, hoping it sounded believable.

And that's exactly what happened. Garrett came to my place at least once or twice a week for eight straight months in a row. Some nights, he would bring dinner over before we made love. He got to know me more on a personal level and I knew he liked what he saw.

One night, while I was at the club with Zach and Skyler, I posted a picture of all three of us, dancing shirtless on a box, on Instagram. Garrett messaged me later that night and did not like one bit of it. He was becoming very possessive of me, getting jealous and insecure of any guy touching me, that wasn't him. I played along and responded back to him, letting him know he was the only man I had eyes for and that I was interested in no other. This response pleased him, and thus, our affair persisted.

I had Garrett Pedrick wrapped around my finger. I had manipulated him into developing feelings for me. And this was only the first pitstop during this manipulation tour I had planned.

Chapter 15

Garrett laid in my bed, naked. His arms stretched behind his head, that rested on my pillow. He held me as my ear pressed against his chest, listening to his heartbeat. I couldn't believe our secret love affair lasted as long as it did now.

Well, actually…I could believe it. I made that shit happen. Duh!

But I was growing more impatient. It took me this long to get Garrett to love me and I had too much skin in the game to back out now. I needed to do more to get involved in Garrett's life. I wouldn't be satisfied until I was able to hang out with him and his friends in public and to meet his husband, Scott.

I had Garrett right where I wanted him. I now needed to push his jealousy buttons a little more and I knew I would be getting my way in no time.

Garrett rubbed my back as we rested in bed. I broke the silence. "So, I've been thinking…" I began with.

"Thinking about what?" He inquired.

"Us. Like if this is all some big mistake," I finished my thought aloud to him.

"What do you mean? Of course, this isn't a mistake. I love you, Logan," he confessed.

"I know. I love you too. But this can't go on forever. I'm young. Eventually, I plan on having a husband and a future with someone one day," I explained.

"No. I get that. I just…I don't know. I'm in a weird predicament," he replied.

"I understand. I'm not asking you to leave your husband by any means, but if we're going to continue this relationship, I can't be boxed in this cage with you," I mentioned.

"What do you suppose we do then?" Garrett asked.

"I have a really farfetched idea, but I'm not sure if you're going to like it."

"Uh oh. I'm not sure I like the sound of that." He chuckled while he replied to me.

"Hear me out. The only way we can continue this together, and you still be with your husband, is if you somehow bring me into your relationship with Scott," I informed him.

Garrett thought for a moment and laughed out loud, uncontrollably.

"That's a good one, Logan!" He exclaimed.

"I'm actually serious about it, Garrett. I'm not saying I'll fall in love with Scott, nor that he would fall in love with me. But maybe if you brought me around more often, we could develop those feelings and maybe we could all be in a throuple, if the cards are right," I elaborated to him.

"Well, how do you expect me to bring you around all of a sudden? 'Hey Scott, this is my friend Logan who I've been fucking for the past eight months behind your back, and I'm now finally telling you about him.' That wouldn't work. Plus, I couldn't even pass you off as a friend. Just look at you. With how hot and sexy you are, he would be completely suspicious and think we were fucking all along."

I shook my head. "You need to get creative, Garrett. You both recently moved into your new house a few weeks ago, right?" I asked.

"Yeah. But what about it?" He wondered where I was going with this.

"Well, do you still need any help with the house? Hiring painters, movers, or something?" I inquired.

"No, we got all of that done already. We have guys coming over in another week to open up our pool, but that's about it," he revealed.

"Well, who's going to maintain the pool? You and Scott?"

"Not sure. I don't think we could, even if we tried," he admitted.

"Well, there you go! You'll need a pool boy. And *I* can be that pool boy," I recommended.

Garrett snickered at the thought. "As hot as that would be to have you as our pool boy, parading around the backyard shirtless for us, do you even know anything about pools?" He asked.

"No. But I can do my research. It can't be that hard. Once I'm motivated and put my mind to something, I can make it happen," I added.

"I believe you. Let me talk with Scott and bring up the idea to him. I think we could make it work." He kissed me on top of my head.

"Yeah. I think we could too," I replied.

"If this is what you want, Logan, I'll do my best to make it happen. I love you and can't stand the thought of not having you in my life," he mentioned.

"Awww, baby. I feel the same way. I can't picture being with anyone else, but you."

I thought to myself. This was a complete fucking lie. I could picture being with someone else besides him. I could picture being with his husband, Scott. And I could picture Garrett being completely taken out of the equation. He was such a fucking idiot!

The plan actually worked! Garrett messaged me, saying he wanted me to swing by their house tomorrow for a fake interview. For the past week, I've been doing my research on inground pool maintenance. I knew of all the necessary chemicals and treatments needed to open a pool and keep it clean and chlorinated. I paid attention and read up on the various plumbing, valve, and pump mechanisms, as well as different electrical panels that some pools use.

I also had a bit of an advantage going into this, because I had Garrett take several pictures of his entire pool, and the pumps for it. I was easily able to compare the equipment the Pedricks had to ones that were online. I could confidently say that I would easily be able to be a pool boy now, with no problems at all.

The following day, I had arrived at their amazing home. It was huge! They could probably get away with having ten other people living there with them, without an issue. This was way too big for only two people.

They needed a third! And I was determined to be that third!

When I knocked on their door, Garrett was the one who actually greeted me.

"Hi Logan! Nice to meet you!" He exclaimed.

I tried my best not to bust out laughing at his poor acting skills, but I needed to play along and maintain a serious and professional demeanor if we were going to make this performance work.

"Yes. A pleasure to meet you too, Garrett," I replied.

Garrett mentioned his husband was in the kitchen waiting for us, and so he led the way. I scrutinized their house carefully. The beautiful furniture, freshly painted walls, etc. I imagined this all would be mine too, someday. I was bemused, thinking about it.

As we turned the corner and into the kitchen, there he was. Scott stood across the kitchen island, staring at me. He was sophisticated as hell! The black polo shirt he sported made him look like a rich golfer, having just arrived home from the country club greens. I instantly swooned.

Garrett interrupted my daydream by introducing Scott and me. "It's great to meet you, Scott," I found myself saying first.

"Well, it's great to meet you too, Logan," he responded. Scott had a perfect, white smile.

What I would do to get a taste of those ivories and lips!

Once again, Garrett ruined my erotic thoughts of Scott with explaining my pool boy expectations, including my schedule. I had to give it to Garrett, he was playing this employer role rather well. Even I was surprised at how specific his details were.

But I soon realized, like me, Garrett was a master at lying. He had been cheating on his husband with me for over eight months straight, and kept it hidden from him this entire time. Plus, who's to say I was the only person Garrett fucked behind Scott's back? I certainly wasn't the first and I probably wouldn't be the last, either. I was on to Garrett. He may have fooled Scoot all these years, but he wasn't fooling *me.*

The thing that was missing from Garrett's Oscar-winning performance was somehow talking me up. I knew he couldn't go too far with giving me compliments or anything. After all, technically, this was supposed to be the first time he was meeting me. If I wanted to mesmerize and seduce Scott, I would need to do it myself, but I would need to be inconspicuous about it.

I thought quick, on my feet. "Do you mind if I head out back and take a look at what I'm working with, and the equipment you have?" I inquired.

Surprisingly, it was Scott that spoke up as I asked this. "Sure. We can walk you out back. Follow us."

Scott and Garrett then escorted me to the backyard. I walked ahead of them, pretending to observe their pool as if it was my first time seeing it. I felt the need to share my faux expertise of pools in order to make my role, as a legitimate pool boy, more believable. "A little murky right now. Will definitely need to give it a shock treatment, followed by a bag or two of diatomaceous earth, depending on the size of the bag you get," I suggested.

Continuing to move ahead of them, I made my way over to the side of the house. I bent over to investigate the main pool equipment and pumps. But I hunched over with a purpose. I arched my back to make sure my ass was sticking out perfectly, for their view. Men found my round, bubble butt irresistible. I knew Scott would have no choice but to take notice of it and I hoped he would ejaculate to the thought of it, later today.

"Alright. Obviously, we will need to purchase the shock treatment and diatomaceous earth, among other chemicals. Scott and I will run out to the store today to pick all of that up. Leave us a list of anything else you think we will need, and we will go ahead and grab it," I heard Garrett say, behind me.

I rose from my bent over position, standing up to face them. "Awesome. Yeah. Would it be easier for me to text it all to you?" I asked.

Of course, I already had Garrett's phone number, but Scott didn't know that. Also, I wanted to take my chances to see if it would be Scott that would provide me his number on the spot.

Both of them were silent for a moment as I requested this, which made things a little awkward, but luckily Garrett broke the ice, and held his phone out to me. "Here. Add yourself to my contacts and then I'll shoot you a text, so you have my number," he stated.

I kept the phone on Garrett's home-screen and pretended that I was typing on it, to make it seem like I was adding my number. Once I returned it to him, Scott chimed in, and handed me his phone too. "In case of an emergency, and Garrett's unavailable, just give me your number as well," he suggested.

Inside, I was jumping up and down for joy. My plan was working, and this could not have gone any better. As I typed in my phone number and added myself to Scott's contacts, I replied, "sure. No problem, Scott."

Seconds later, my phone buzzed, and I saw a notification pop up on my screen, indicating Scott had sent me a text message: ***Scott Pedrick. This is my number.***

It was official. I was now the Pedricks' personal pool boy, and I could not be more thrilled about it. All was going according to plan. This whole scheme was coming to fruition. I seriously considered myself a fucking genius for making this shit happen.

I was halfway there to accomplishing my goals, I set forth. I had managed to seduce Garrett. Now I needed to get Scott to bite. Although I would be working with the pool *pipes*, I was looking forward to working with *Scott's pipes*, more.

Chapter 16

It had been a full two weeks since Scott and Garrett hired me. I was over their house four days a week, working on their pool, for the most part. Being a pool boy really wasn't that hard of a job, much to my surprise.

Even after my first visit to the Pedrick house, Garrett still kept coming over to my apartment for our usual sexual rendezvous. Garrett was in greater spirits when he visited. He mentioned that he felt confident that our plan would work. Garrett admitted that he and Scott had sex last week after a discussion about me, and that he knew that Scott thought I was sexy as hell.

Fuck yes!

I was over the moon to learn that Scott was attracted to me already. I can't say that I was surprised though. That's just how I was. I could make men fall for me at the snap of a finger. Call it a gift. Call it a talent. Call it whatever you will. But it always fucking worked.

Garrett came up with a brilliant idea. "We are actually having a house-warming slash pool party in two weeks. All of our gay friends are coming over. You should too," he informed me.

Hmmmm. A gay pool party? Right up my alley! Now that's what I'm talking about!

"Yeah. I think that would be awesome! That'll allow your friends and Scott to get to know me more, on a personal level," I explained.

Garrett kissed me, glad that I was on board with his suggestion. "Everyone will fall in love with you, just like I did. Plus, they will get to see you in a speedo. What's not to love about that?" He smirked.

I jokingly hit him with my pillow. "Well, who says I'm wearing a speedo? What if I decide to wear normal swimming trunks? Hmmm?" I asked.

Garrett held his hands out toward me, in an attempt to deflect the blow from my pillow. "All I'm saying is, it would be a real shame if you didn't show off that amazing body to everyone. You worked so hard to get it. Not to mention, you would have Scott drooling over you," he pleaded.

Of course, Garrett was right. There wasn't a chance that I would be showing up to a gay pool party in anything but a speedo. And, it would specifically be my navy, blue speedo that I would be wearing, the same one I had in my Instagram thumbnail photo. Garrett had also shared with me that he witnessed Scott's reaction, in looking at my Instagram profile picture for the first time, resulting in him practically shooting his load in his pants at the very sight of it.

So, showing up to the Pedricks' place in this same exact speedo was the optimal choice, that would allow Scott to see my perfect body that he *oh so* admired.

"And don't mention that you know anything about the pool party to Scott when you come over our house, before then. I think it should be left as a surprise. Also, maybe you should come an hour or so after everyone else arrives. It would be hot if you made a grand entrance in front of everyone, in your speedo." Garrett started snickering as he mentioned this. "Our friends are going to be so fucking jealous when they find out that you're our pool boy! They won't be able to keep their hands off you," he added.

After Garrett and I finished mapping out this whole elaborate plan of my attendance at the pool party, I decided that I would make sure to never go shirtless or wear speedos at the Pedrick house, up until that day. I needed to make Scott wait and linger. It was already confirmed that he saw a picture of me in a speedo on Instagram, so I figured I would torture him with not being able to see my full body, in person, until then.

God, I was so fucking bad! And I loved it!

I pulled onto the side street of Garrett and Scott's house. The last thing I wanted to do was park behind everyone else in their driveway and wind up having to come back outside to move my car again, to let them out from being blocked in. I knew that everyone else would be leaving the party long before me.

How did I know that? Well, Garrett planned for me to spend the night. He would also make sure that it would seem like he and Scott were both insisting that I stay over, pressuring me to enjoy the party and drink more. I was hopeful that this would actually work out, because if it did, there would be a potential chance that I would also be getting fucked by Scott tonight. If I played my cards right, there would be a threesome with Scott, Garrett, and me. And I was determined to make that happen sooner, rather than later.

I decided to leave my bag of belongings in the car. It would be a little presumptive of me to bring a lot of my items into their house. Plus, I wanted to make sure nothing was holding me back from when I showed off my body, walking across the yard to meet everyone. I checked myself in the mirror of my car one last time and adjusted my hair, before putting on my navy sunglasses that matched my speedos. I pulled off my sweatpants, so that I was on full display ready to make the entrance.

Garrett had mentioned that he wanted me to enter the backyard from the far back gate. So, I did as he recommended and made my way over there. I stood in front of it with my hand on the handle, ready to open it.

Here goes nothing!

I entered the yard and began slowly strutting my way across the freshly cut lawn. The walk seemed like the length of an entire football field. I could see that everyone was in the lanai, so I headed in their general direction. I was giving my best, Gisele Bündchen catwalk, staring straight ahead through my shades, as I trekked across the backyard with swag.

When I was about halfway across the yard, I could start to see the heads turn. The gay men were watching this young, hot model grace their presence. Ever should they be so fucking lucky, to have me in their company. I had every single man's cock hardening as they eye-fucked me, and I was loving every minute of it.

When I was only a few steps away from everyone, I could see Garrett making his way over to me. He placed his arm around me. I could smell the booze on his breath. He must have already been drunk. "Hey, everyone! This is our new pool boy, Logan!" Garrett announced.

Really Garrett!? That's your best introduction of me!? Fucking idiot…

I waved *hi* to everyone as Garrett dragged me right over to Scott, bypassing everyone else. Scott had a blank expression on his face. I knew he was completely distracted by my thick legs, round chest muscles, abs, and the bulge in my speedos. His eyes were aiming right down at my lower body and not up at my face, which is exactly what I was hoping for.

This was my first time seeing Scott shirtless, and I loved what was in front of me. His chest was so thick and hairy. It turned me on so much.

I took off my sunglasses and went in to hug him. His body felt so nice, up against mine. I knew he was not expecting this, but I definitely wanted to keep surprising him. "Hey, Scott. Thanks for having me over."

I withheld my laughter, knowing he was shocked that I was here right now. It was hilarious to watch him squirm. "Oh. Of course. Glad you could make it," Scott replied.

Before we could even start a conversation, Garrett had already made his way back over to us, pushing a shot on me, which was perfect. It was exactly what I needed right now. Something to take the edge off of this whole experience. However, I wouldn't let them know that by any means. I played it off as if the shot was too strong for me and that I needed to pace myself.

"I think I'll start off with a beer. Don't want to get too crazy, since I have to drive home later."

I fucking hated beer! Bleh!

But it was a sacrifice I was willing to make to keep up this whole charade. I needed to pretend I was responsible and didn't want to drink anything heavy, with the idea that I would be driving home later in the evening. Hopefully, Scott was enjoying this performance and character I was portraying.

I felt Garrett smack me on the back. "Ahhh! Don't worry about that! We have four guest bedrooms you can pick from if you need to stay the night. Don't hold back!" He yelled.

I shrugged and let them know that I would consider their offer. However, I could see that the vultures had now swooped in and were behind me, wanting to join in on the conversation. I decided to play nice with these homos and talk with each of them that approached me.

Most of them were fairly nice, trying to get the scoop on who I was, what I did, and how I met Scott and Garrett. Every one of them also asked if I was single. Not really surprised that they did. Who fucking wouldn't?

After several conversations with these guys, I decided to get another drink and make my way into the pool, to get my body and hair wet. I dipped my head in the clear, cerulean, blue water and popped back up, slicking my hair back, purposefully.

I emerged from the pool and sat in one of the empty lounge chairs on the side, that was available. I put my sunglasses back over my eyes and tried to relax and work on my tan, while taking the time to think about my next move. I needed to find a way to get someone to talk me up to Scott. It wouldn't be enough for him and Garrett to just have discussions about me. It would have to be one of his friends that could speak nicely about me to him. Hell, it would be a bonus if his friends told him how irresistible I was and recommended him and Garrett come on to me.

My time to reflect more on this didn't last very long. I saw a shadow cast over me and opened my eyes to see that it was Pete. He was thick and had a bit of a stomach on him. Not my type at all. He sat in the chair that was next to me. I knew exactly who he was. After stalking Garrett's Instagram for the past year, I practically learned everything about Pete in advance. He was a doctor like Scott, and he was married to Lyle, who was also at the party. However, he didn't know that I had already acquired this information. So, I would need to act like it was my first time ever having seen him.

"Logan, right?" He asked.

"Yeah. And you are?" I waited for his response.

"Pete. Nice to meet you…again," he added.

"Oh? We met before?" I had a shocked look on my face as I said this.

It was the only thing that happened so far at the party that I didn't expect. I was pretty certain I had never met Pete before. Maybe he was mistaking me for someone else. If he was, then I would be pretty fucking offended. No one was comparable to me.

"Yeah. I bought you a drink at the bar several years ago. You told me your name was Cody, though," he revealed.

Fuck! How could I be so fucking stupid and careless!?

I vaguely remember him now that he mentioned it. However, I would try to play it off as if I had no idea what he was talking about.

"I'm not sure I remember that. Maybe you're thinking of someone else?" I asked.

"No. It was definitely you. I couldn't forget a face and a body like that," Pete answered.

Was Pete hitting on me? Ewww.

Ridiculous. He was flirting with me even when his husband, Lyle, was here. I rolled my eyes underneath my sunglasses when he said this. But then I started thinking…maybe I could use Pete to my advantage. He would be gullible enough to think I was into him. I simply needed to get the right angle and leverage. Then, I could use him as my little pawn. He could be the one to talk me up and tell Scott he should consider a three way between him, Garrett, and me. This would actually be perfect!

"Now that I recall, I think I do remember you. And you're right. I probably did tell you my name was Cody. My bad. I don't like strangers to know my real name. There are a lot of crazies out there. Do you know what I mean?" I explained.

"Yeah. I completely understand. Look, I know I have a husband and all, but damn boy. What I would give…" Pete stopped himself from finishing that line.

I smiled at him. "Mmmm. I wish we could find a private place around here. I'd blow your mind," I teased.

"Oh yeah? Well, I think we could arrange something. I'd have you blowing more than just my mind," he retorted.

"Hot! So how do we get alone?" I inquired.

"Easy. A lot of people will probably start to leave in the evening. We can both purposefully be the last ones to get out of the pool and dry off. We'll go upstairs and get changed. Then, I'll sneak into whatever room you're in. Leave the door cracked, so I know which one you're in," Pete explained.

Damn! He was conniving as hell!

I admired it. It was smart. I underestimated him. I decided to add an improvement to his ploy.

"That works. Make sure you wait five minutes before you come up. People will get suspicious if you leave to get changed the minute I do," I recommended.

"Of course. I planned on doing that to begin with. This ain't my first time at the rodeo, boy," he responded. "Anyway, I'll catch you then. See you later, sexy." Pete got up from the chair and moved away.

Now, I had a strategy in place for Pete that would have him easily wrapped around my finger. I only had five minutes of peace before someone else came over to me.

For fuck's sake! These guys were on me like flies on shit!

This time, it was Scott who approached me. He was the only guy at the party that I didn't mind talking to now. I was glad to have this chance to speak to him, privately. We could get to know each other over the flow of the drinks.

"So, hopefully our friends aren't causing any trouble for you?" He asked.

"Oh no! Not at all! Everyone's been nothing but nice to me. You have a good group of friends," I lied.

Your friends are a bunch of boring ass cheaters. Even junk mail was more entertaining than them. Your stock is plummeting. Time to find new investments!

That's what I really felt like telling Scott, but I kept my judgments to myself. Scott started to ask me questions about where I went to school, what I was studying, and how long I'd been a pool boy for. I appreciated that he was asking me these questions. It meant that he was interested in getting to know me. I too asked him about his job, although I already knew all there was to know about it.

Our getting to know each other was interrupted by Garrett, stumbling over to us with two shot glasses.

Garrett was really fucking with my game here. Just whose team was he on!?

"Here! You both have been slacking on me!" Garrett exclaimed, handing Scott and me the shots that were in his hand.

I continued to play up the polite, responsible role I started earlier. "I'm not sure if that's a good idea. I don't think I'd be able to drive home if I took one more," I explained.

Garrett slapped me on the leg when he heard me contemplate taking the shot.

Jesus! Garrett must have been really drunk. He was getting handsy with me in front of Scott! What the fuck, Garrett!?

He soon redeemed himself. "Of course, you can have another shot! Our offer still stands. You can stay the night if you can't drive home. Right, Scott?" Garrett turned to his husband as he asked this.

"Yeah. Feel free to stay over if you need to, Logan," Scott stated.

Never mind. I take it back. Garrett knew exactly what he was doing! Despite that he was drunk as hell, he was still able to keep his eye on the prize. Like he mentioned earlier, he was making it seem as if it was partially Scott's idea to make me want to stay the night. I had to give Garrett some credit. I honestly should have never doubted him to begin with. After all, we were two of a kind. He's a liar and a conniver, just like me. I would be stupid to forget that I reminded myself.

It was going on 8:00pm, and just as Pete had predicted earlier, most of the guys at the party were heading out. There were only a handful of people that were choosing to stay longer. Most of the other gays were already heading inside and getting changed. I chose to sit outside, still. I glanced over to see that Pete still hadn't gone inside yet, either. So, he really was willing to go through with this.

Seeing that only one other person was outside with us, I decided now would be a good time as ever to head upstairs to get changed. I entered the house and found myself in the kitchen. Only Lyle was present there, munching on some snacks. "Hey Logan! Everyone's downstairs. We're gonna get karaoke going. You want to do the first duet with me!?" Lyle was annoyingly excited.

Poor schmuck! He was attempting to be kind and friendly to me, not knowing I was about to have sex with his own husband. Oh well…can't be helped.

"Sure! I need to change into dry clothes, but I'll meet you downstairs in a bit," I replied.

"Awesome! You good with a Journey song?" He questioned.

"Yeah. Hit me with any of them. I should be good."

Lyle left the kitchen walking towards the basement doors. I soon headed upstairs with my bag of clothes. I decided to go into the guest bedroom that was furthest away from the main stairs. The wallpaper was sage green with a matching bed spread. I pulled out a bottle of lube from my bag and tossed it on the bed. I stripped down naked, throwing my navy, blue speedo to the floor.

I grabbed my phone and turned the camera on, switching it over to video mode. I hit the red record button and placed my phone on the nightstand, next to the bed. I leaned the phone against the back of the box of tissues that was there but made sure the tip of the phone was visible, so the camera lens could get a full image of the bed. I propped myself on the bed and got on all fours, facing the wall. Two minutes later, I heard the door to the bedroom shut behind me.

"Fuck yeah, boy! You ready to take my dick!?" Pete whispered in a deep, aggressive tone.

I turned my head to see that he was stripping down. "Hell yeah! I've been craving that cock all day," I pretended.

I held the bottle of lube up to him. He grabbed it from my hand and started slicking himself up with it. I felt the chill of the lube run down my ass as he poured it on me and rubbed my hole with his finger.

"Let's make it quick, before anyone comes looking for us," I recommended.

"You don't have to tell me twice," Pete replied.

I felt his half-hard dick rub up and down my ass until it was fully erect.

"You ready for it, boy!?" He asked.

"Yeah. I fucking need it bad!" I begged in desperation.

Pete pressed his dick deep in me and started fucking me, relentlessly.

I began to moan and grumble with pleasure, but he put his hand over my mouth wanting me to be completely silent.

"Fuck yeah! Take my fucking dick! Take all of it!" He said, a little more loudly than he should.

Then, less than a minute later, he started grunting, slowing down his rhythm.

I turned my head to face him. "Did you…?"

He finished my thought for me. "Yeah. I came." He pulled his cock, that was now flaccid, out of me.

That was fucking fast! I mean, I know I told him to make it quick, but I didn't think it would be that quick! How fucking anticlimactic! Literally!

Pete proceeded to put on his clothes. "Damn, boy! That was hot! That ass was the tightest…" he started off saying, before I interrupted him.

"Yeah. Now, let's get down to business," I abruptly said.

"Business?" Pete had a perturbed expression written on his face.

"Yes. Business. I need you to do me a favor," I declared.

"A favor? That depends on what it is."

I went over to grab my phone from the nightstand and stopped the recording.

"Well, it actually doesn't depend on what the favor is. You will do me any favor I ask or else I will share the video of you fucking me with Lyle and I'll post it online too."

Pete's eyes widened as I revealed this. "You fucking little shit! You wouldn't dare do that anyway, without having to expose yourself too!"

"I can easily edit my face out. Not hard to do," I clarified.

"Who the fuck are you!? Is your real name even Logan!?" He asked.

"Yes. It actually is, but let's get to the point, here. You're wasting my time," I folded my arms across my chest as I said this.

"Fine! What's your stupid, fucking favor!?" Pete demanded to know.

"It's actually not that big of a deal, honestly. I need you to pull Scott aside. Say some positive things about me. Tell him how sexy you think I am and convince him that he and Garrett should have a three-way with me," I revealed.

He shook his head. "Are you fucking serious!? Are you that sex hungry!?"

I dangled my phone in my hand, in front of him. "I don't need to explain anything more to you. You either accept it or you don't. If you accept, I'll delete the video. If you don't, it gets blasted out tomorrow, all over Xtube, Pornhub, Xvideos, you name it!" I threatened him.

Pete let out a sigh, realizing he didn't have much of a choice here. "Fine. I'll do it. But listen to me. You better stay out of my fucking life after this! And Lyle's too! You got it!?"

I devilishly grinned and nodded to him. He finished putting his clothes back on and stormed out of the room. Now that I had Pete as my little minion, doing my dirty work, I was more confident than ever that I would have Scott Pedrick fucking me, before the night was over.

It was like I told Garrett a few weeks ago when he wondered how I would learn how to be a pool boy: *Once I'm motivated and put my mind to something, I make it happen!*

And I was determined to make Scott Pedrick and me *happen*!

Chapter 17

That night, after the pool party, Scott, Garrett and I fucked for the very first time. It was one of the most passionate, sexual experiences of my life. I could not get enough of Scott Pedrick! Even if it meant I also had to have sex with Garrett and him at the same time, I would be willing to commit to that. Any reason to be able to get fucked by Scott was reason enough for me.

I made sure to bring myself around them, more often. The three of us fucked multiple times a week and hung out almost every day. Everything was working out the way it should! I kept our *friends with benefits* relationship building up for the next three months. I knew both Garrett and Scott had developed feelings for me. I could also sense the jealousy they now had if any other guy were to give me attention or flirt with me.

It was now time for me to force Garrett and Scott to take that next step with me, with Garrett's help of course. I would need to make Scott realize he didn't want our relationship to end, meaning he would want me to be in a throuple with them.

At dinner one night, I made up this whole elaborate lie about how some guy named Austin asked me on a date and that I was considering taking him up on that offer. Garrett played the *jealous boyfriend* role rather well. Even I was convinced by his acting skills. Between my plot and Garrett's charade, it worked! Eventually, Scott and Garrett revealed to me that they didn't want me to date anyone else. The three of us were then officially in a *throuple*. On Christmas Eve, they asked me to move in with them, by giving me a key to their house as a gift. Things were all going according to plan!

I was at the home stretch. Now, I was unsure of whether or not I could get rid of Garrett. At least I now had Scott, no matter what. I was fairly pleased to now be a part of this wealthy lifestyle with them! I would really have to hone my deceptive skills if I wanted to try and drive a wedge between Garrett and Scott, so that Garrett would leave us, and I could have Scott all to myself. I couldn't believe how far I've come! There was no way I would simply try and settle for this throuple now. I was a determined man!

In the many months we lived together, I decided that I really had to up my game, if I wanted to try and find a way to drive Scott and Garrett apart. What I truly needed was some intel and dirt on Garrett. He lied to Scott about so much already, I knew that there had to have been more that he was hiding, even from me. So, when I finally had the entire house to myself, which was extremely rare, I took complete advantage of the opportunity. I snooped through Scott's computer in the office and tons of paperwork in the desk drawers. It was full of financial information and other boring shit, nothing that was compromising.

I then found Scott and Garrett's medical records. Scott was as healthy as an ox. Garrett on the other hand had AFib. That, I already knew. Nothing that was a revelation. However, something did catch my eye that I didn't know. Garrett's allergies. Apparently, he was allergic to bees, and Sulfa-based medications. I read further along and saw that his *on-set symptoms* included *breaking out in hives* and *trouble breathing*. So, whenever Garrett took Sulfa-based medication he had breathing trouble.

Well, that was interesting to know. I heard the garage door slam, which caused me to put the papers back in the drawer and quickly delete the browsing history on Scott's computer, so they didn't know I had been on it. I emerged from the office and came into the kitchen to greet Garrett, who had arrived home, first. He came forward to kiss me and then dragged me upstairs to have sex with him.

Garrett was still jealous, even though I was now in a relationship with him and Scott. He made us all promise that we would only have sex if the three of us were all together and present. Secretly, I knew his reasoning behind this. It was because he was insecure about Scott fucking me. I wasn't sure specifically why he would be insecure about it. It had to have been one of two options: The first, was that he was obsessed with me and wanted no one fucking me unless it was him, or unless he was present when Scott and I were having sex, with him being involved. The second, was that he feared me and Scott having sex without him would somehow make Scott love me more and put him on the outskirts. I wasn't sure which of these options made him insecure more. Hell, maybe it was a combination of both.

Garrett was starting to become more trouble than he was worth. Even his attitude over the past few months had changed. He acted like a little, spoiled rotten, piece of shit, anytime he didn't get his way. I hated when he got like this. He was so fucking selfish, and unworthy of Scott's love.

He was a loose cannon. I needed to get rid of him fast, before he wound up blowing everything up in my face. And the only way to get rid of someone fast, while being innocent in their disappearance was by making *accidents* happen.

Even though I was now more determined than ever to somehow kill Garrett, this wasn't the first time I had these thoughts. They had been recurring for the past several months. However, I was smart in how I looked into ways of killing him. I was leaning towards the medical route. Garrett had AFib and I now learned that he was allergic to Sulfa-based medications, from what I gathered in snooping around the house. If I could somehow mix a concoction of some sort with a dose of medications that were lethal to him, then maybe everyone would assume he died of natural causes, strictly related to his AFib.

If medical examiners, investigators, or police did suspect foul play, they would undoubtedly look to Scott, right? He was the cardiologist. Scott knew all about Garrett's medical history. Not me.

However, this would be the worst possible outcome, but I was confident that it would never come down to this. I would need to be as furtive as possible in how I made this *accident* happen.

To begin with, I decided not to search on my phone or personal laptop about anything related to AFib or Sulfa-based medications. Investigators could easily search my device history and it could be an implication. I needed to do this research on a public computer, that they would never be able to trace. I've seen enough Dateline NBC episodes and crime television shows to learn these methodologies.

I went into an empty computer lab in my college, in between two of my classes during the day. I sat in the back row in the corner of the lab and logged onto the computer as a guest. I began searching through medications that people with AFib should not take. These medications would increase the chance of the victim having a stroke: Any blood thinners, such as Aspirin. Your typical NSAID pain relievers, like naproxen and ibuprofen. Certain antibiotics, the worst being Bactrim and Azithromycin (or the Z-pak).

I could get the blood thinners and NSAIDs over the counter, but I would need a prescription to acquire anything else. I filed this in the back of my mind, as I closed the internet, deleted the browsing history, just in case, and logged off the computer.

Chapter 18

I thought I would at least have to get a little dirt on my hands to try and drive a wedge between Garrett and Scott, but Garrett was doing one hell of a job, himself.

What a fucking schmuck!

Garrett's personality took a turn for the worse. He bitched about everything. It was always his way or the highway, and he threw a tantrum if things didn't go like he had planned.

He was acting like a spoiled fucking brat. It was the most unattractive thing I'd ever seen in my entire life. Even when we went to Greece and Turks and Caicos, he was constantly trying to argue with Scott and me over the craziest things. I had never seen anything like it. And it was only getting worse!

The most annoying part about it was that Scott let him get away with this shitty behavior! He would let it go and ignore him most of the time.

Scott was just as guilty for enabling it!

It had now been a full year since I met Scott and our relationship with each other had grown astronomically since then. Our attraction to one another, the personal and meaningful conversations we've had, and even the sex had increased and improved greatly. He and I would be so much better off if Garrett was out of the picture.

He needed to go ASAP!

I knew it wouldn't be long before Garrett would completely fly off the handle. He just needed a little push to get there, and I had a genius idea that might be able to get the job done!

I became more aware of Garrett's insecurities. He hated when Scott and I were around each other without him, and he hated when Scott and I agreed on things that he didn't necessarily agree on. So, it was time for me to push Garrett's insecurity buttons to the limit.

I was only one year away from getting my bachelor's degree in Human Services. I lied to Scott and told him that I desperately needed some field experience before graduating, but that I wanted an actual paid position and not an internship. I went on to explain that all of the human resources and management offices I applied to were only willing to hire me as an intern. I falsely told him that none were willing offering me a salary. So, I suggested coming into Scott's Cardiology Office and working as one of his front office managers.

This would be a win-win scenario for me. Not only would it give Scott and me some alone time away from Garrett, but it would drive Garrett fucking bananas!

Also, I knew I would be getting extra brownie points with Scott. He had practically begged Garrett to work in his office with him for years, but Garrett continuously outright refused those offers. The fact that I would be willing to do it without any cause for complaint, would paint me in an even greater, positive light to Scott. He had to take notice of this and draw comparison with how I was so willing to help him at his office and work with him, while his husband, Garrett, was being a selfish, nasty fucker about it.

Scott didn't have to reflect on it much. He agreed with me, that it was a wonderful idea. We sat down and planned my work hours around my college classes. I would start heading into the office next week. "So, are you going to be the one to tell Garrett, or do you want me to?" I asked. Deep down, I knew there was zero chance I would be breaking this news to Garrett. I knew Scott would inevitably be the one to do it, but I wanted to fabricate and show my willingness to be the one to break the news. Scott would appreciate the gesture, I thought.

"Nah. I'll do it later today. He'll completely understand," Scott predicted.

Ha! My ass! Did Scott really think Garrett would react so calmly to the news!?

Well it wouldn't be long before we found out.

"So, you two are going to work together now, leaving me hung out to dry!?" Garrett yelled, not handling the situation well, at all. That evening, Scott informed Garrett that I would be working with him at the practice.

Just as I had anticipated, Garrett threw a huge temper tantrum over it. "You still don't get it!? This has been going on for the past few months. You and Logan are getting closer and closer, while you and I are growing apart!" Garrett confessed to Scott.

I really needed some popcorn for this. I would just need to sit back and let Garrett go at Scott. He was showing his true colors and revealing all those insecurities I knew he had buried inside him. He was completely threatened by me and I was fucking living for it!

After some bickering back and forth, Garrett decided that he would be heading out. Scott chased after him. "Where are you going now!?" He yelled to him.

"Out. Don't bother calling me. I won't be home until later tonight. I need to vent," I heard Garrett announce, before he left the house.

Scott came back into the family room to sit with me. "I swear! It's always something with him!" He said with vexation.

Scott was right. There was always something wrong with Garrett, and I knew exactly where Garrett was going. He was heading out to fuck one of his tricks. How easily Garrett forgot that I was one of his tricks in the past. He would always show up at my apartment door after he and Scott got into a verbal altercation. He decided to take his aggression out, by fucking me. So, I had no doubt he was doing the same thing right now, except with some other random guy.

I actually didn't give an ounce of a fuck as to where Garrett was going. He made one fatal error, which was leaving me alone with Scott, after getting into an argument.

Big fucking mistake, Garrett! Big fucking mistake!

Scott sat on the sofa next to me, completely distressed by this entire situation. I knew Scott was completely vulnerable in this very moment. I couldn't let this opportunity go to waste.

I placed my hand on his back and started to slowly rub it, hoping it would calm his nerves down. "I'm sorry, Scott. It's not your fault. Really, it's mine," I proclaimed. I tried to sound as disheartened as possible.

I felt Scott's hand linger on my thigh, clenching it. I loved anytime I felt him touch me, as if he owned me. He did own *me*, and I would allow him to. "No, Logan. It's not your fault. This is not your fault by any means. I'm sorry that you have to deal with it. It's one thing for me to have put up with it for years, but it's another thing to have dragged you into it. And now, you have to tolerate it too," Scott admitted.

I was surprised Scott was being this open with me, right now. He was more vulnerable than I had imagined. I could tell he was not in his normal frame of mind.

I continued to sympathize with him. "I don't mind tolerating it…I really don't." I said.

"And that's why I love you, Logan. You are completely unselfish, thoughtful, caring, and sexy as hell, of course. You're everything. You shouldn't have to put up with this bullshit," Scott confessed. I felt the warmth of his hand cup my cheeks, while he stared into my eyes.

He wanted me so badly. I could tell.

It was my turn to open up. If I let him know how deeply I cared for him and let him know my love for him superseded my love for Garrett, then he would respond so well to it. He had to hear this. "No. I know I don't have to put up with it. But I do it all for you, Scott. I am madly in love with you. I can't lie to myself. If you left this relationship, I don't think Garrett and I would last very long together. But if it were only you and me, I would still be head over heels. I still feel that way about you to this day and always have since we first got together," I asserted.

Scott said no words after I shared this with him. He moved in and started kissing me, wildly. His hands were moving up my shirt to feel my body.

Scott wanted to fuck me. He wanted to fuck me alone!

This was finally happening. It had been long overdue. Scott grabbed my hand and escorted me upstairs to our bedroom. We snatched each other's clothes, yanking them off. I positioned myself flat on the bed with my arms behind my head, seductively. As Scott moved closer to me, I released one of my hands to cater to his thick cock. His moans indicated that he was pleased with what I was doing, so I moved closer to him to get a taste of his dick. I began blowing him slowly and methodically. I lived for Scott's cock. I wanted to please him so much. I knew he felt the same about me. There was this unexplained magic between us. It was beyond intense.

I felt Scott's dick tightening as he picked up the pace, fucking my mouth. I locked my eyes with his, as my lips curled around his shaft. Scott lost control whenever he saw me sucking his penis, with my eyes glaring up at him. It turned him on so much. I knew exactly what I was doing. Suddenly, Scott pushed me back, off of his dick.

I wiped my mouth with my arm and smirked. He didn't want to cum this early. He wanted to fuck me in the ass. He wanted to fuck me hard and cum inside me. He wanted to *own* me.

I rolled across the bed and grabbed the lube, letting him know I was ready to take him. All of him. I lubed myself up and then his cock. I flipped over to my stomach, so I was facing the headboard of the bed. I propped myself up on all fours, and arched my back as much as possible, sticking my ass out, giving him the perfect angle of it.

Scott took the reins. He slid his tip inside me, but refrained from pushing his entirety, deep in me. I gasped loudly at the mere touch of it. But I was hungry for more. I wanted all of him pounding me. What was he waiting for?

"Come on, daddy. Fucking give it to me. Please…" I begged.

He pushed it all the way in as I finished pleading with him. I yelled as the full-length of his dick plunged deep in me. I slammed my face down hard, into the pillow and closed my eyes, feeling the pleasure of that warm cock of his, sliding in and out of me.

"Fuck yeah, boy. That's it. Take daddy's dick! You can handle it. Come on!" Scott roared in a deep voice.

This is what I wanted! What I've been fucking waiting for!

Scott's true sexual desires were now unhindered without Garrett being a distraction. He was enraptured with me, sexually, physically, and emotionally. I had managed to work Scott over. And now, that he was picturing what it would be like to have me to himself with no one else involved. He was loving it! He wanted more of it and wasn't willing to go back.

He continued to ravage my hole. I couldn't get enough of him. His hands gripped my hair and pulled my head up with great force, out of the pillow. His dominance was intense, and I was made for it! "Fuck me, daddy! Fuck my hole deeper! I want you balls deep in me!" I screamed like a sex-craved maniac.

But he pulled out of me to my astonishment. I turned around, not only annoyed, but bewildered too. I was starving for his cum, but he didn't give me what I had wanted. "Why did you pull out!?" I asked.

"I want to see that face of yours when I cum. I want to see the look on your face as you squirm knowing I'm breeding you raw!"

Fuck yes!!! Scott was a savage! A fucking sexual beast!

I submitted to him, turning to lay on my back. He lifted my legs in the air, before they rested on his shoulders. He pressed his cock into me once more. I moaned in delight, feeling him back inside my asshole, right where he belonged.

I could feel his hands clamp down on my shoulders and push his dick into me, more and more. I closed my eyes, enjoying every second of it. However, Scott wasn't having it. "Open your eyes…" he said with assertion. "Open those fucking eyes! I want to look into those fucking eyes when I cum in you!" He demanded.

I did as he instructed. I opened my eyes, staring right into his. The longing for me and my body was written on his face. It was hot! I was getting close to cumming. "Fuck, Scott! You're gonna make me shoot, babe!" I shouted.

Then, Scott did the unthinkable. He wrapped his hand around my throat and squeezed, pounding my ass relentlessly. He was choking me. I fucking loved it! The sight of his masculinity controlling me, and him taking what was rightfully his, put me right over the edge. "Fuck daddy! Right there! Oh my god, I can't hold it any…Arghhhh!!!!" I yelled as I combusted. My load shot all the way up my chest and behind my head.

The visual was enough to make Scott ejaculate into me. "Yeah baby! Take it all! Take every fucking bit of it!" He thrusted as deep into me as he could when he came. He fell on top of me once he finished.

We rested, trying to regain our energy. Little did we know our moment of post-sex bliss would be put to a pause, as I heard a grungy, obnoxious sounding voice.

"And what the fuck is this!? Are you fucking kidding me!? I knew it!!! You fucking liars!!!" Garrett shouted.

Scott and I rolled off each other and sat up in the bed, facing Garrett who was now standing in the doorway of our bedroom.

He glared in my direction. "And you…I don't know who the fuck you think you are! I brought you into this relationship! And I could easily push you right out of it, so don't fucking try me!" He threatened.

My eyes widened in horror. It was all over with, I thought. He was going to reveal everything to Scott. We would both go down together.

All of my hard work over these past two years for nothing!

Luckily, Garrett stopped right there and didn't proceed any further. My worry began to subside, but still lingered in the back of my mind.

Garrett was out of control. But he wouldn't hurt me, like that, would he? I stood up, moving closer to him, to grab his hand, trying to appease him. He instantly pushed my hand away. "Don't fucking touch me! You filthy fucking slut!" He screamed at me.

"I'm done with this shit. I'm sleeping in the guest room tonight. You two can continue to fuck each other like monkeys all you want now, since I won't be in bed with you tonight. That's what you really wanted all along, right!?" Garrett continued to yell.

Eventually, after the argument went on, Garrett finally did wind up going into the guest bedroom, slamming the door behind him. It left Scott and me to sleep alone and cuddle together in our master bedroom.

As I laid in bed that night, panic began to strike.

How could I be so fucking stupid!?

I knew my goal was to get Garrett worked up and push him out of this relationship, but I had no idea his emotions would run off the rails like this. Nor did I consider that he would have the audacity and balls to expose our past, secret love affair to Scott. I seriously thought that would be the end of it tonight. And it was a pretty close call.

There was absolutely no way I would be willing to give up this life I now had: this house, Scott, the vacations and perks that came with being with a rich doctor. All of it! And I certainly wouldn't let a dirty, undeserving whore like Garrett be the one to take it away from me.

There was only one option that would prevent any of this from happening. I considered it for the past few months, but it had to be now or never. I cringed at the thought of it, but it needed to be done.

I had to kill Garrett! It was now or never!

Chapter 19

I woke up and checked my phone to see that it was already 9:00am. Garrett had caught Scott and me making love in Garrett's absence, the night before. I placed my hand over my forehead. I still had a headache from all of the screaming that occurred last night. Not to mention, I knew things would still be tumultuous throughout the entire day, with Garrett still being unhinged.

In the not too far off distance, I could hear our garage doors open and close. Curious as to who was heading out the door this early, I sprung out of bed and made my way downstairs in my underwear.

I entered the kitchen and saw Scott standing there. I walked over to him to give him a kiss. "Good morning, babe," he greeted me.

"Good morning. Was that Garrett that left? I heard the door shut," I asked.

"Yeah. He went for a quick run," Scott explained.

Perfect. This gave Scott and I alone time to talk about everything that transpired last night. I thought it would be in my best interest to play the victim role here, to make it seem like Garrett's anger was the result of my actions and decisions. I wanted him to believe that I was second-guessing our entire relationship. It would make him desperate to do anything to keep me here, with him. "Oh…okay. Listen. I wanted to talk to you more about last night. Do you think this whole thing is a mistake? That we've been moving too fast?" I asked.

"What? No. Of course not, Logan. I don't want you to ever think that. Look. Whether you were here or not, Garrett would be like this. That's just who he is. It has absolutely nothing to do with you. I was actually glad that you came into our lives when you did. And now, I can't picture my life without you, Logan," Scott admitted to me.

That was music to my fucking ears!

It was exactly what I was hoping to hear from him. Scott never wanted me to leave. He couldn't imagine me not being a part of his life. I was doing backflips on the inside. I continued to talk with him about Garrett's behavior last night. I chose my words carefully, making sure I wasn't being completely cruel to Garrett, but that I wanted to help him. That he needed help to control his emotions and volatility. Once the discussion between Scott and me came to a close, I felt the need to get myself cleaned up and together. After all, I was only in my underwear, not that anyone would seem to mind, especially Scott. I'm sure if he had his way, he would make a house rule that I was *only* allowed to be naked when we were home.

"I'm gonna head upstairs and get showered for the day. Okay?" I let him know.

"Yeah. Sounds good," Scott replied back to me.

I paraded upstairs and tossed my underwear in the clothes hamper in our walk-in closet. I turned the shower on and waited for the water to heat up, before stepping in. I could feel the warmth of the water strike every surface area of skin on my back. It was soothing to the touch. I dipped my head under to get my hair wet and stood there for a while, enjoying the heat and relaxation it gave me.

I shampooed and conditioned my hair, before grabbing a washcloth and soap to clean every toned muscle on my body, along with every crevice, created by my sexy curves.

My focus on my body was interrupted as I saw the steam from the shower escape, now that the glass door was opened. I was surprised to see Scott was standing before me. Was he in the mood for some hot shower sex?

"Hurry. We have to go, Logan. Garrett's in the hospital!" Scott announced.

What the hell!? What the fuck was going on!?

"Oh my god! What!? What happened!?"

I immediately hopped out of the shower, grabbing my towel to dry myself off with.

"The cops said a neighbor found him passed out on the sidewalk, from a stroke or heart attack," Scott revealed to me.

How was this possible!?

"Holy fuck, Scott! I hope he's okay!" I said with concern, although deep down, I was skipping for joy.

"Me too, Logan…me too."

An hour later, Scott and I were in the hospital, waiting to hear from the doctors about how Garrett was doing. A former colleague of Scott's came in to greet us and then brought us into a private room.

He made the difficult announcement to the two of us. "I'm sorry, Scott…Garrett didn't make it. There was nothing we could do. The stroke left him brain dead before he arrived at the hospital. And by then, it was too late…" The doctor confessed.

Garrett…was seriously dead!?

My emotions were mixed. On one hand, I was deeply saddened and couldn't believe this had actually happened. On the other hand, this was the cherry on top of the race to the finish line. I had made it! Scott and I would no longer have to be tormented by that fucking, nasty piece of shit, Garrett. We were free, and I didn't have to get any blood on my hands in the process!

Scott began to cry. The omen the doctor had revealed was permeating through him. I too put on my best expression of shock and horror and broke down with Scott. Dr. Nassim left the room to give us time to digest this entire thing.

Scott wrapped his arms around me and held me. We both cried together, mourning the loss of Garrett. Well, at least one of us was.

Chapter 20

I couldn't believe it. I had actually gotten away with everything.

I seduced Garrett and inserted myself into his life. I kept my fake interest in him up for eight months, with the intent of getting into a relationship with his husband, Scott Pedrick. I was able to get Scott to develop feelings for me and make him want me to be a part of a throuple with him and Garrett. Then, I was able to expedite Garrett being on the outskirts of our relationship.

The only part of the plan I hadn't carried out, that was a surprise, was Garrett's death, which happened long before I had anticipated. The best part about it was that I didn't have to kill him myself! He died on his own! He went for a long run, while he was out of shape, and overexerted himself into having a stroke.

What a fucking schmuck!? An irresponsible bimbo!

Garrett had provided me with the greatest gift of all, which was Scott falling right into my arms. I had to be patient with being excited about Scott and me now having the opportunity to move forward with our lives together. It had only been several days since Garrett had passed. I had to act extremely upset. I had to make it seem like I actually loved Garrett and that him passing was a complete loss for me.

Instead, it was actually a complete fucking gain for me!

The day of the funeral had arrived, which was extremely awkward for Scott and me, but mostly me. Neither Scott's family nor Garrett's family had any clue as to who I was. It would be beyond ridiculous to explain our relationship to them now, at this very moment in time. So, I decided to hang in the shadows and fade into the background during the entire funeral.

A lot of our gay friends did approach me to express their sympathies and condolences. Surprisingly, Lyle sat with me most of the time.

After I blackmailed Pete at the pool party last year, I was forced to have to hang out with the two of them more, now that I was a part of Scott and Garrett's lives. I decided to apologize to Pete, privately, letting him know I simply had this bizarre sexual fantasy of wanting to fuck Scott and Garrett badly and that I was so attracted to the thought of it. Eventually, he gave in, and forgave me. I'm not sure if he really wanted to forgive me, but he had to, knowing I would inevitably be in his and Lyle's lives for the foreseeable future, since I was in a throuple with Garrett and Scott.

As Lyle and I talked, I saw Pete and Scott out of the corner of my eye disappear, for a bit. I honestly didn't think anything of it. Being insecure and worrying about my past antics coming back and biting me in the ass was something I let go of the minute Garrett died. I had covered up all of my tracks carefully and strategically. I made zero mistakes, and now, I could continue on with my life and with Scott, living happily ever after.

A few minutes later, Pete and Scott came back into the main room. Scott was now heading in my general direction. This prompted Lyle to get up. "I'll be back," he stated, stepping away from me.

Scott now took the empty seat next to me, on the sofa. "How are you holding up?" He asked me.

I gave the deepest sigh of sympathy that I could muster up. "I'm okay for now, I guess. A lot of our friends came up to me, to show me support. That was really nice of them. How are you?"

"I'm okay. Listen…I had an idea. I've actually been thinking about it for the past two days. Once things settle down, why don't we take a vacation together? We need an escape from the house. A change of pace and a change of scene would do us both good. How does that sound?" Scott suggested.

I was a little taken aback by this. I couldn't believe Scott was thinking about this right now, at his own husband's funeral. But I was all about it! Scott was trying to move on rather quickly and he wanted the two of us to have a good time together, privately. So, I couldn't judge him too harshly for this. However, I still felt the need to maintain the victim card for myself and pretend to still be sad that I had lost one of my lovers. "That sounds like a nice idea. But let's talk about it later. I feel a bit guilty having this conversation here, right now," I recommended.

"No. That makes sense. Anyway, I'm glad to hear everyone is treating you well and making you feel better. I'm gonna head back up front with the family. Come get me if you need anything," he let me know.

Scott gave me a caring smirk. It made me aware that he wanted to kiss me or touch me right now, but we both knew that would be a terrible idea. I simply smirked back at him to let him know I understood how he was feeling.

The funeral proceeded normally, just as any old funeral would. Boring as fuck.

It wasn't until we all were outside, when I physically saw Garrett's casket get lowered into the ground, that I could finally return to breathing normally. That was it for Garrett. It was time to keep him in the past, right where he belonged.

It had been nearly two weeks since Garrett's funeral. I still had a role to play. I couldn't just jump into Scott's arms and move on with our lives right away. That would be too suspicious. I needed to continue to mope around the house for a while and feel upset and bitter about Garrett's death. Scott and I did go out on romantic dinner dates, a few times, but nothing came of it. I made sure we only had sex once in the past few weeks.

I decided to wait until our vacation to Cancún, Mexico, to start letting him fuck my brains out as much as he wanted. That would be a good starting point to *moving on with our lives.*

It was two days before our flight to Mexico. Scott was out of the house running errands for most of the day. I figured I would take this time to surprise him and take care of all the packing for us. I pulled out our suitcases and placed them on the settee in our bedroom. I went ahead and packed Scott's belongings first, starting with his shoes, shirts, and pants. Then, I went for the main items that were in the drawers, in his walk-in closet, including underwear and socks. As I opened Scott's sock drawer, I realized he had nothing but black socks in the front. He had to have at least some nice, colorful dress socks, right? He couldn't be that much of a drab.

I pulled some of the black socks out, tossing them on the floor, which allowed me to see a lot of his other socks that were hiding in the back. As I grabbed another pair and put them on the ground, I heard a jangle come from them.

That's weird…

I dug my hand into the sock to see what the hell was in it. As I snagged the items out of it, I was blown away by what I had discovered. They were three orange, unprescribed pill bottles labeled Celecoxib, Meloxicam, and Oxaprozin.

I had never heard of any of these medications before in my life. I found myself grabbing my phone and searching online to see what they were. As I Googled them, I had wondered why Scott had these medications concealed in the back of his sock drawer.

Did he have some medical condition he wasn't telling me about? What the hell was he hiding?

I continued to search the internet for any information about these drugs. The only commonality they had was that they were strong prescription NSAID medications, usually used to treat extreme neck and back pain. But Scott didn't have any recurring pain to my knowledge. He was completely healthy. And if he did have neck or back pain, why would he feel the need to keep that from me? Why would he keep these drugs in the back of a sock drawer?

Then it hit me, like a car striking a deer in headlights. I had remembered where I saw *NSAIDs* pop up recently. It was when I was at my college, researching medications that people with AFib should be wary of taking.

These medications increase the risk of causing severe strokes for those who were diagnosed with AFib. I placed my hands over my head in disbelief as I was putting together these puzzle pieces.

No…it couldn't be. There's absolutely no way!

It was Scott. Scott killed Garrett.

I couldn't believe it. I didn't want to believe it. But I knew I had to. I hurriedly put the pill bottles back in the socks and tucked them away in the back of the drawer where they once were. I cleaned all of the other socks up and closed the drawer.

My next reaction was to return all of Scott's pants, shirts, and shoes back to their respectful places. Then, I put the suitcases back into the closet. I didn't want Scott to think I started packing some of his clothes, because he may get suspicious and think I had dug through his sock drawer and knew about the medications. There was no way I could confront Scott about this. It would have to be my secret to carry for him. And I would carry it with me to the grave.

Chapter 21

Scott and I were now laying on the beach, soaking in the sun. I held his hand as we stared out into the ocean. After I discovered that Scott had murdered Garrett, I didn't care about it one bit.

Scott had killed for me. And if he didn't kill for me, then it would had only been a matter of time before I killed for him.

He killed Garrett so that he could start his new life with me on a clean slate. He was obsessed with me. He loved me. The fact that he risked getting caught for murder to be with me, said everything. Scott was my fate, my destiny. He was meant for me and I was meant for him. I too would have killed for him.

I would never let him know that I knew he committed this act though. I kept it to myself, in fear that he would think me knowing about it would ruin our relationship, and that was the very last thing I wanted to happen.

As we enjoyed each other's company on the beach, Scott informed me that he had a surprise for me for this evening and that he had dinner arrangements already planned out. As we got back to our hotel room from the beach, we both freshened up. He was the first to get in and out of the shower. As I got my shower afterwards and came out to dry off, I noticed he was waiting on me. "Why don't you head down to the hotel bar and grab a drink, babe? I don't want to keep you waiting on me," I suggested.

"You sure?" He asked.

"Yeah. Go for it." I stepped forward to kiss him on the lips.

"Love you, babe," he responded to me after I kissed him.

"Love you too," I replied.

Scott left the room and headed for the elevator down the hall. I went over to the closet to pull out the clothes I would be wearing tonight, which would be the sexiest gray pants I owned, that made my ass look fucking delicious, and a white button-down shirt that made me absolutely irresistible.

After all, Scott was giving me a huge surprise tonight, right?

Wrong. Well, technically, he thought it would be a surprise, but it definitely wasn't a surprise to me. I knew Scott would be proposing this evening. I was a snoop after all, so what did he expect? Before we left for our vacation, I rummaged through his suitcase, hiding some sex toys in there for us to use, during the trip. Then, to my surprise, I discovered a tiny black box that had a white gold ring in it with diamonds encased around it. The ring was my size, and it fit me perfectly.

So, I knew Scott's plan for this trip. Nothing ever got past me. But needless to say, I was floating on cloud nine right now, as I gelled and combed my hair in the bathroom mirror. In less than one hour, I would be engaged to Scott Pedrick. I would be Logan Pedrick in the near future. Or maybe he would be Scott Rippling? It didn't matter to me either way. I smiled at myself in the mirror, thinking about it.

All of my hopes and dreams I had for myself were finally coming true. Even a pool boy can have dreams.

Epilogue

Scott

Garrett had stepped too far. He was a miserable son of a bitch for the last few months that he had left to live. Once Logan Rippling came into the picture, I completely changed. I had never been obsessed with someone in my entire life, the way I was obsessed with him. I had never experienced these sorts of feelings for anyone, ever. Not even with Garrett.

I couldn't explain it, nor did I know how to describe it. All I knew was that I wanted Logan all to myself. He was my destiny. I *owned* him and I didn't want anyone else touching him, loving him, or hurting him. Garrett was already checking two of these three boxes. However, once I realized his nasty fucking attitude was upsetting Logan and hurting him, I knew I couldn't let him get away with it.

I had accepted Garrett's poor behavior for a while now, but it was time to put that to an end. Whenever Garrett and I were both having sex with Logan, it took every nerve in my body not to push Garrett off of him or punch him for touching and making love to Logan.

I was turning into a controlling, mad man. Garrett was preventing me from having Logan all to myself. I couldn't stand it any longer.

So, there was only one way for me to remove Garrett from this entire picture, and that was to kill him.

I no longer loved Garrett. I only loved Logan. So, in my eyes, Garrett was now my enemy, competing for the only man I loved. And only one of us could remain standing and be with Logan. *It had to be me.*

However, I had to make Garrett's death seem like an accident. It was his AFib that would be my key in this entire scheme. I needed him to have a heart attack or a stroke. That way, his death would be instantly linked to his AFib. For the next several weeks, I replaced Garrett's AFib pills with prescription NSAIDs. It would only be a matter of time before these drugs would work on him systemically and lead him to his death.

It was Garrett that pushed himself to this limit. While he was on these NSAIDs and taking a long run, his poor heart wouldn't be able to take it. And that's exactly what happened. He suffered from a stroke right on the sidewalk in front of the neighbor's house. The upper chamber in his heart was so clotted, the clot inevitably travelled to his brain and caused the lethal stroke.

Now that Garrett was gone, Logan and I could start our new lives together as a couple. Three was a crowd and there was only room for two to play this game.

Keep Reading for an Excerpt from the Cul-de-Sac

BY BJ IRONS

Skyler

June 22nd, 2019

“Fuck…Daddy at one o’clock!” I lowered my sunglasses to get a clear view of the shirtless jogger making his U-turn around our cul-de-sac. That’s when the blood rushed to both my brain and my cock. An immediate hard-on grew through my skimpy, seafoam-green swim-suit and I didn’t give one ounce of a fuck who saw. I can’t even think of a way to describe him: Achilles, Zeus, Giorgio Armani model? Something Italian or Greek and hot! It’s beyond the imagination…but not beyond my imagination of wanting to get a feel of that body. I’d already had thoughts about him several times since he and his equally hot husband moved into the neighborhood less than two months ago. Thoughts not only about them individually, but what I would do to be in a spit-roast sandwich between those two pieces of…

“Seriously, Skyler!? He’s like at least ten years older than you!”

Boner kill!

I could sense the heavy eye roll of my twin sister, Celeste, as she laid spread across the chaise lounge next to our pool in our backyard, with a clear view of the street from the side, soaking in the sun through her SPF 8 sunblock. She firmly believed any SPF above 15 would completely prevent the development of a tan, and she spoke so confidently of it as if she were an actual dermatologist. I knew she was just as much of a slut as I was, but she always had to put up this façade in front of people. It didn't matter whether it was her friends, my friends, or strangers around us. She could never be her true self, which annoyed the hell out of me, because it seemed as though she propped herself up on this dignified pedestal and left me down below. At any rate, I never called her out on it. I've seen the anger and wrath of Celeste, and today was not one of those days I was willing to push her buttons to bring that side out of her. I knew how to pick and choose my battles.

"Oh, come on, Celeste! Don't be so vintage! And besides, we all know how Skyler gets when he sees a new bright and shiny toy." Zach was right beside me as he poked fun at me. In my periphery, I caught him checking out the jogger as well. There was no doubt that Zach was attracted to the new Mr. and Mr. Rogers in the beautiful neighborhood. He just didn't open up about it as much. As coy as a Japanese fishpond that one tried to be. But it was total bullshit. I knew Zach better than that and he too was putting on a prudish show in front of my sister. But I had to chuckle. How ironic that out of the six houses in our court there were now a total of four gay guys! Zach and I, and the hunky new couple in their mid-thirties that just moved in, Lucas and Bennett.

Clearly this was a two versus one battle right now and I loved being the minority in an argument.

"I'd watch your mouth, Zach. A little birdy did a kiss and tell recently. I heard all about the 'shiny new toys' you and he used just last week at the after party of…"

"Fuck off, Skyler!" I could hear the annoyed grit in his voice. God, I loved getting under Zach Cauderling's skin. It was a game I was always willing to play and getting that reaction out of him was a constant mental orgasm. Maybe it was my way of boosting my own ego and bringing down his. Don't get me wrong, Zach and I are great friends. We have a history together and our families have one as well, strictly platonic of course. We grew up together since kindergarten.

I came out of the closet my senior year of high school and went through hell for it. However, having the front and center striker of our varsity soccer team protect me and constantly have my back was something that I could never forget. Zach made a lot of sacrifices in high school by choosing to sit with me at lunch and hang out with me. He risked his teammates and everyone else in our school making up rumors about us and our relationship. But he didn't care. Zach was mister popular. He was the trend-setter, and everyone looked up to him. Star athlete and AP student.

Of course, it was a major shock to me when he too told me that he was gay during his sophomore year of college. I didn't know what to think of it. Part of me wanted to be able to fulfill those high school fantasies and fuck the shit out of him – or rather get fucked by him – now knowing he was gay and that I stood a chance. Meh. I'm pretty versatile, so both. The other half of me appreciated that he came out to me before anyone else and I took into consideration our history and all that he had done for me. So, I never really thought about taking it a step further with the fear of things not working out and completely ruining our friendship.

That was only a year ago. Now, we're both juniors in college. Our relationship has since turned into more of a friendly rivalry. When we went out to bars, nightclubs, etc., we always shared and compared our conquests, for the most part. We even resorted to challenges that were always refereed by Celeste: Who could wind up with the most drinks bought for them by the end of the night? Who would win the wet underwear contest that night at the club? Who wound up with the most dollar bills in their socks and underwear while we flaunted our shirtless selves on separate boxes stroking our hands across our abs as we swayed to whatever popular club remix was playing at the time? We loved pretending to be go-go dancers. Admittedly, it was pretty much 50/50 as to who would win.

Hmmmm.

I ran my hand across my chin now that the cogs in my head were turning. Our friendly little skirmishes were always short-term during a single night out. Why not raise the stakes a bit? "So, what do you think of the new guys in the neighborhood?"

Zach's laser-like focus on the hot jogger subsided. His brown locks swiftly moved as he turned his head towards me. "What do you mean what do I think of them? They're nice guys."

God, he was so fucking annoying sometimes. Could he just for once be a little more open about his sexuality? He's made his rounds around town and out of town with a lot of college guys. There should be nothing for him to hide from me, especially with me being an open book to him.

But I knew Zach was thinking about sex with the new neighbors. I know his facial expressions all too well, and I could tell when he was eye-fucking somebody, like he was moments ago. He didn't realize he had revealed his poker hand to me, so now it would be easy for me to place a bet against him and win. I ran my hand through my bright blonde hair. "Care to make a wager?"

At this point, Celeste took off her white Prada shades and placed them on the side table next to her glass of rosé, before making her way to the side of the pool, realizing she was about to reprise her role as referee. "Here we go again…" She submerged herself into the crystal blue water.

I caught Zach's smirk out of the corner of my eye. That look on his face always made my insides melt. He gave this same look whenever he was entertained by an idea. Those pearly whites glistening in the sun. You could tell he practiced this look in the mirror more than once and he knew it made him irresistible. Cocky son of a bitch. But I knew he was intrigued, and I now had his full and undivided attention. He took the bait, but not graciously. "Really, Skyler? How many times is it going to take for you to lose and be embarrassed to give up on these little challenges of yours? I mean, when is it ever going to be enough?"

Damn it. I hated when he did this. He was reversing the roles and he knew that I wouldn't let any condescending comment slide. The stubbornness gene was definitely on the same chromosome as the gay gene. "Ugh! You're so full of shit! You never beat me. In your wildest dreams!"

"Well, clearly, you need to be put in your place. So, what is this challenge you had in mind?"

"Let's be honest. You and I both can't deny how sexy the new neighbors are. We both wouldn't exactly turn them down if they ever came on to us."

Zach squinted as he was attempting to figure out where I was going with this. "Yeah? And your point?"

I grabbed my can of fruity hard seltzer and took a giant gulp before revealing my ultimate scheme. "Well, let's make it a race. Which of us can seduce one of them fastest?"

Zach let out a heavy belly laugh, almost spilling his beer. "You can't be serious, Skyler. This one is a new low…even for you!"

I shrugged, signaling my dismissal at his remark. "I mean, hey, I completely understand if you're intimidated. I would be too if I were in your shoes." This prompted Zach to sit up in his chair. The tension in the air between us was almost tangible.

"Alright. I'll bite. So, what are we competing for this time? And don't say any of your fake designer sunglasses and accessories. They have Canal Street written all over them."

That bitch!

Only some of my sunglasses, wallets, and shoes were fake. A majority of them were real. Besides, how would he know anyway? I caught my sister pursing her lips ever so slightly as she leaned against the edge of the pool listening in on our conversation, and that pretty much answered my question. So much for twin secrecy. I can't tell that whore anything. Duly noted.

"No. That's too amateur. Hmmm..." Then it hit me. Taking away Zach's two greatest possessions, his ego and dignity, would be the cherry on top of a win. "I got it! The loser has to text the victor a sincere and authentic compliment every day for the rest of the year!" I held out my can of spiked seltzer to Zach. The sound of his beer bottle then clinking my can was like music to my ears. Zach was going down. This game was going to be way too fucking easy. I had it in the bag.

He took a swig of his beer again shaking his head. "Skyler, you know this isn't even a contest, right? Just because you get over a thousand likes from strangers on Instagram only puts you in the minor leagues. Those two guys across the street...it's going to take a lot more than pictures and videos of you twerking to get their attention. I don't think you have what it takes."

I gave him the heaviest eye roll of my life behind my green sunglasses, but I didn't flinch. I didn't want to give him the satisfaction of seeing me squirm and get irate. I spoke nonchalantly. "Too bad I don't care what you think. All you need to worry about is starting to rehearse some of those compliments. And I forgot to mention that there can be no repeats. Each compliment has to be different every day."

Zach reclined in the lounge chair. "You really do think you can seduce one of them, don't you? Haha. I have to admire you. It's a little cute. Just remember you can't throw thirty gay hashtags their way to get them to notice you. #gay #gaytwink #gaydude #gaysofinstagram…"

My teeth were gritting. Now he was pissing me off. I hated when Zach got like this. It was one thing to be competitive, but Zach took it to a whole other level. I get he was trying to have fun and he knew I could handle his sly remarks, but sometimes his teasing could just be plain mean. It was one of the only things that I found unattractive about him.

"Listen, Zachy-poo. You talk a big game, but you better…" I was interrupted by Celeste's heavy grunt as she stepped out of the pool and flopped herself down in the lounge chair very dramatically. But I can't say I was surprised. That's who Celeste was. She acted as if a live camera feed was on her 24/7. She wanted her life to be like a reality television show. Hell, I think I'm actually guilty of the feeling too. Call it a twin thing.

"Can you guys just bang already? My god! It makes me want to fucking vomit!" She grabbed her sunglasses from the table and allowed the white Pradas to conceal her hazel eyes before she grabbed her rosé by the stem, swirling it. "You two are so disorganized. But thankfully you have me here to make sense of things."

Zach and I both raised our brows at her as she continued to remain on her soapbox. "You both can't go after each of them. One of you needs to attempt to get in Lucas's pants, and the other with Bennett. You need to be a little more focused about it."

I had to give it to Celeste. Her words made complete sense. If Zach and I both went after Lucas and Bennett at the same time, our contest would probably be obvious to them. Plus, we would wind up derailing each other's progress. It was Zach who acknowledged

Celeste's idea and concurred. "So how should we decide who we go after?"

It seemed that Celeste had an answer to this too. "I have a spinner app on my phone." She tapped on her cellphone to unlock it, holding it in our faces to show us what she was referring to. "I'll just add both of your names in here like this..." Zach and I exchanged smirks with one another as she typed. "And poof...now we spin the wheel. Whoever's name the arrow lands on, that person will be targeting Calumny Court's very own infamous, shirtless jogger, Bennett. Sound good?" We both nodded and eagerly sat on the edges of our chairs as we heard the ticking of the wheel spinning. The ticks slowed until it was silent. Celeste lifted the device in her hand high to the sky. "And our lucky winner is... Zach!" And sure enough, the arrow was pointing to the blue part of the wheel that showed Zach's name.

I shook it off. "It's not like it matters anyway. I would be fine with either or. But there you have it. I got Lucas, and Zach has Bennett. Let the games begin!" Unbeknownst to Zach, I'd already had private conversations with Lucas since they'd moved in. I knew I had the upper hand going into this.

And just like that we were off to the races. It was now only a matter of whose cock would cross the finish line first.

Acknowledgements

Thank you, Matt and Ed, for being my rocks during this writing experience and tolerating the sex scenes I read aloud to you many a times to get your opinions on.

Cate, I owe it to you for dealing with my constant text messages and emails back and forth about this work. You did nothing but heighten my creativity and motivation on completing this novel.

Peter, my editor, you have been an amazing person to work with and only helped my work reach new heights. I am so looking forward to continue working with you on future projects!

And thank you to my mother Gina, brother Jimmy, and the rest of my family and friends for your love and support. If you're reading this, then I'm absolutely mortified that you read this entire book and the carnal scenes that came with it, but I warned you!

Most importantly, thank you to the LGBTQIA+ community. I will continue to support my community and give us more fun reads in the near future!

About the Author

BJ Irons works in the field of education.

Many of his personal experiences as a gay man have contributed to this book.

This is his second novel.

Being a part of the LGBTQIA+ community himself, BJ hopes to continue to bring more positive fictional works to his LGBTQIA+ readers.

Follow BJ Irons on Instagram:

Made in the USA
Middletown, DE
04 June 2021